"You can't hold me captive!"

Savannah continued desperately, "It's a felonious imprisonment."

"Actually," Dexter mused, "I'd prefer to call it a job opportunity."

"This is kidnapping!"

"And what you tried to pull off is fraud."

Savannah bit her lip. Her career could be destroyed. A reporter who lost her credibility wasn't exactly hot property.

"All right. I'll stay. If I can write the whole inside story of your life...."

Dexter stared at her. "You have the gall to negotiate with me? Remember, Savannah— you haven't seen revenge, yet. But believe me, you're going to!"

Dear Reader,

This book started with a dream about a heroine who first meets her hero when she wakes up in his arms. It's the first time I've turned an actual dream into a story.

But it's not the first time my dreams have become reality. For years, whenever I could steal a moment, I escaped into another world, where my characters patiently waited. I wrote, rewrote and burned a quarter of a million words. Then one day Harlequin Mills & Boon published my first book.

Whatever your dreams may be, I wish for you the feeling I had that day—the wonderful confidence that dreams come true.

Leigh Michaels

P.S. I love to hear from readers: you can write to me at P.O. Box 935, Ottumwa, Iowa 52501-0935, U.S.A.

TAMING A TYCOON
Leigh Michaels

Harlequin Books

TORONTO • NEW YORK • LONDON
AMSTERDAM • PARIS • SYDNEY • HAMBURG
STOCKHOLM • ATHENS • TOKYO • MILAN
MADRID • WARSAW • BUDAPEST • AUCKLAND

ISBN 0-373-03367-2

TAMING A TYCOON

Copyright © 1995 by Leigh Michaels.

First North American Publication 1995.

CHAPTER ONE

THE glass-enclosed office near the top of Chicago's Metro Tower was normally an island of peaceful quiet, but at the moment Savannah wasn't enjoying the atmosphere. It was funny how much things could change in the blink of an eye; only a minute ago she'd been feeling just fine. But then the editor of *Today's Woman* had tossed a manila folder down on the desk between them and said, "Sorry, Savannah, but I don't think we can use this." And everything changed in the flick of an eyelash.

Savannah looked unbelievingly up at the editor's face, and then down at the slim folder, lying so innocently on the blotter. She knew what it contained—a long, detailed, elaborate magazine article, a story she had spent weeks researching and putting together. And now the magazine's editor said he couldn't use it?

She shook her head a little as if to clear her hearing. "You said you wanted a profile of Dexter Caine, Brian."

"I said it sounded interesting," the editor corrected. "And it still does. But frankly, as you've written it . . ." He shrugged. "There's nothing new here."

Savannah bit her lip and then said reasonably, "It's the best information available about a man who's never been exactly easy to pin down. I dug into sources you wouldn't believe, Brian."

"No doubt. You're a meticulous researcher. But this is really no different from the piece you did on Caine last year for the *Tribune*."

It *was* different, and Savannah could show him a dozen bits of information that hadn't been available last year.

5

But before she could decide which example to use first, Brian opened the top drawer of his desk and tossed a tabloid newspaper toward her.

Savannah recognized the shrieking headline and the grainy, slightly out-of-focus photograph that made Dexter Caine look like a gangster. There was another copy in the tote bag at her feet, part of her file on Dexter Caine.

I ought to have known that piece of so-called journalism would give me a whole lot of trouble, she thought.

"Your story doesn't even mention the newest bit of gossip," Brian said.

"The Cassie King controversy?"

Brian's gaze narrowed. "You've read the *Informant*, then?"

"I'm not an idiot, Brian. I know that even a trashy gossip rag like the *Informant* can sometimes stumble across a real story. But there's no evidence they've gotten things right this time. I checked that story out, and there's no proof it's true."

"Can you prove it's false?"

"At this moment? No. But my gut feeling—"

"Well, if we go with your gut feeling and ignore it, and about the time our story appears Dexter Caine marries Cassie King, we'll look like fools, won't we?"

"You'd look even more foolish if you ran a piece speculating that he'll marry her and then he doesn't," Savannah muttered. "I tell you, Brian, there's nothing to that story but a few hints dropped by Cassie King and her publicist. You know what stars are like—any news coverage is better than none, and if there isn't a legitimate story to push, they'll make one up just to get media attention."

"Yes, I know. Still, that doesn't mean there's nothing to it. So I'm afraid we can't use this piece just now. The magazine's lead time is too long, and anything could happen by the time that issue comes out. Sorry,

Savannah, but unless you can get the inside story and add something new..."

"Something new? Like what? It's going to be awfully hard to prove Cassie King's lying."

"You could get a comment from Dexter Caine. If he'd go on the record about his relationship with Cassie King, we could publish. Then even if he changed his mind and did the opposite, we'd be covered."

Savannah ran a hand through her long blond hair in frustration. "Brian, be realistic. You know the man hasn't talked to a reporter in donkey's years. For all I know, maybe he never has."

"Well, that leaves us with a problem, doesn't it? Now if you'll excuse me, Savannah, I've got a magazine to run. Thanks for coming in."

Savannah stood up, but she wasn't finished fighting. "What about a kill fee? I knocked myself out on that article."

"Sorry. I really am. But you did the piece on spec, and I can't pay you a cent for it unless I use it."

Savannah nodded wearily. "Because if the other free-lancers heard of it, they'd want the same deal. Brian—"

"That's all I can do, Savannah. If you're interested, I could use a piece on lead poisoning. There seems to be a problem with some imported ceramics."

"Oh, that sounds exciting. It's on spec, as well, I suppose?"

Brian's voice was gruff. "Write me a quick-and-dirty proposal of how you'd approach the subject, and I can probably make it an assignment. Pay on delivery of the finished piece."

Savannah sighed. Brian was doing the best he could; he didn't owe her any further work at all. It wasn't his fault that she'd let herself count on the fees from the Caine article to pay her next month's rent. That was her own shortsightedness.

"I'll take a look at lead poisoning and let you know," she said.

She kept her smile in place till she reached the elevator, then slumped into a corner while she rode down to street level.

It wasn't that Savannah hadn't gotten used to rejection; she had. She'd learned in the past two years that the odds were heavily against a free-lance journalist. For every sale, it seemed there was at least one article that never paid a dime, and usually a half-dozen ideas that fell apart during research and never even got to the writing stage.

But Savannah had thought she'd found the inside track at *Today's Woman*. The last four pieces she'd proposed had sold, and Brian had been fascinated when they'd talked about Dexter Caine just last month.

Besides, the Caine piece was *good*. Savannah had done her homework, and she was a talented writer who could turn a difficult subject into a highly readable article. And Dexter Caine was certainly a difficult subject.

It was a perfect September day with just a hint of autumn crispness in the air, and Michigan Avenue was busy as always on Friday afternoons. As closing time approached, shoppers bustled from store to store along the Magnificent Mile.

Savannah shifted her tote bag to the other shoulder and headed toward an outdoor coffee shop just across the street from the Metro Tower. She'd take a break and then go to the library. She had a couple of ideas that needed more research before she could present them to an editor; that was why she'd lugged her laptop computer along on this trip downtown. She could at least look around for another place to sell the Caine article. And while she was at it, she might as well find out what had been published recently about lead poisoning. A whole lot, she suspected. Finding a new twist was going to be a real challenge.

Darn Cassie King and her inconvenient timing anyway, Savannah thought. If the woman just hadn't picked this month to delicately hint that after a five-year relationship, Dexter Caine was finally going to marry her...

Of course, every tabloid in the nation, and a good part of the serious press, as well, had jumped on that particular bandwagon. Cassie King was a gold-plated singing star, with a dozen number-one hits in the past few years, so anything she did was apt to be news. And as for Dexter Caine—well, when a man had avoided attention for as many years and through as many billion-dollar deals as Dexter Caine had, the least hint of information was apt to be treated with the same attention as an announcement from the Archangel Gabriel, whether there was any truth to the story or not.

In this case, Savannah would bet the rent money she didn't have that there wasn't a shred of fact involved. She couldn't put her finger on why she was so certain, except that Cassie King occasionally told terrific stories that didn't turn out to have happened the way she said they did. Besides, in Savannah's opinion, if Dexter Caine actually wanted to marry the woman, he'd had more than enough time to do so. He wasn't the indecisive type; when Dexter Caine made up his mind to do something, it got done.

Savannah wondered what he thought of all the hoopla. He could save himself a lot of annoyance if he'd talk to the press, she thought. Not the press as a whole, of course; that would be overdoing it. But if he'd give his side of the story to one sympathetic reporter, it would end most of the wild conjecture....

Right, Savannah, she told herself dryly. And I suppose you think you're the sympathetic reporter he should choose!

She finished her cappuccino and started down Michigan Avenue toward the library. No matter how annoyed Dexter Caine was, the interview of the century wasn't going to happen, so she might as well get on with real life and see if she could find a way to pay her rent.

Besides, maybe the man *wasn't* annoyed. He might not even deign to notice the press speculation about him and Cassie King. He'd ignored a good many similar things in the past few years.

The library was a half mile from the Metro Tower, and the leather-look vinyl shoulder bag Savannah carried was heavy. Her laptop computer weighed only ten pounds, but as the blocks went by it seemed to grow heavier. She could hail a cab, of course, but she had a better use for the few dollars the ride would cost. Besides, traffic was slowing down. Either rush hour was starting early tonight or there was an accident or an obstruction ahead. Walking would probably be faster, she told herself.

She shifted her bag to the other shoulder, crossed the Chicago River, and trudged on.

It wasn't long before she saw what was slowing traffic. A black limousine, its windows too dark to see if anyone was inside, was double-parked on Michigan Avenue. A uniformed chauffeur leaned against the driver's door, arms folded across his chest, face impassive, ignoring the annoyed comments of drivers who had to squeeze into the one remaining southbound lane to pass.

A big shot, Savannah thought. Or—more likely—someone who only thought he was important.

The car was parked directly in front of a corner building, a century-old structure with Italianate moldings, rounded corners, and elaborate arched windows. It wasn't one of Chicago's most striking or famous, and if she hadn't noticed the number gold-leafed above the main entrance, Savannah would have paid no more attention to the building now than she ever had before.

But she recognized the number from the research she'd been doing in the past month. This building was one of a multitude that Dexter Caine owned, and it was one of the main hubs of a business empire that stretched across the country and around the world.

She remembered being surprised when she'd stumbled across this address, buried in an obscure little business publication. She wasn't startled that Dexter Caine had business connections in Chicago; he had them in a dozen cities, so why not here? But an old building on Michigan Avenue seemed a strange place for Dexter Caine to choose for his American headquarters. A shiny, sleek, glass-and-steel tower in Manhattan—now that would have made more sense.

But it seemed he hadn't built himself a monument anywhere. Instead, he'd bought buildings like this one.

Savannah paused on the sidewalk and looked up at the seven-story brick-and-terra-cotta facade. The building was a sturdy, unpretentious example of the first so-called skyscrapers, built just after the great Chicago fire of the 1870s when the city's builders invented a new style of architecture. The structure was pretty enough, and it appeared to have been meticulously cared for. But it wouldn't land on anybody's list of most important buildings in the city.

And if she hadn't remembered the number, there would have been nothing to give her a clue. There was no name on the door, no neon signs, no logos—just the number.

And, of course, the limousine in front. Did that mean—*could* it mean—that Dexter Caine was here?

What did she have to lose by walking in and asking? Maybe he wanted to talk to the press—but it was a sure thing he wasn't going to call Savannah Seabrooke and invite her over to have a chat. On the other hand, if she just turned up and asked if he'd like to air his side of the story...

She'd get thrown out, that's what would happen.

Well, she'd had worse experiences. And at least then she could tell herself she'd tried everything. What kind of a reporter was she anyway, if she didn't seize the opportunity—no matter how much of a long shot it was— to save her story?

She pulled open the heavy plate-glass door before she could talk herself out of it.

The lobby was at the precise center of the building. It was larger than she would have expected from the age of the building. It was also bright; from a skylight seven stories up, golden sunlight cascaded past brass-and-iron balcony railings to warm the marble floor of the lobby. Savannah paused for an instant to admire the effect— gleaming polished brass, dark twisted iron, gray and black marble. They were all hard surfaces, and yet the lobby wasn't cold and indifferent.

Of course, it wasn't precisely warm and welcoming, either. A young man was standing at an octagonal marble desk in the center of the room, studying her over a heavy brass rail. "May I help you?" he asked. His voice wasn't precisely unfriendly, but he sounded as if he had his doubts that he could be of service.

Savannah wished she'd stopped somewhere and looked into a mirror. Her hair must be windblown from her walk, and she vaguely remembered running her hands through it in Brian's office. She wished she'd put on a dress for her interview instead of her usual, more comfortable garb—boots, trimly cut designer jeans, and a soft, dark blue wool blazer. She wished she'd taken that cab after all; at least she'd have been cool and collected....

No, she didn't wish that, for if she'd been riding by in a cab she wouldn't have paid attention to the building's number, and she wouldn't be here now.

She stepped up to the desk with a confident smile. "I'm here to see Mr. Caine." Her voice echoed a bit in the huge space.

The young man didn't betray by the flicker of an eyelash that he'd ever heard the name.

"Mr. Dexter Caine. My name's Seabrooke." Savannah lowered her voice a little to diminish the echo, but she kept her tone firm. She'd learned early in her journalism career to make statements, not ask questions, in situations like this. For one thing, to make a request implied that the person being asked had the power to refuse permission, while the statement seemed to say that authority had already been granted.

Besides, she hadn't said she had an appointment. If the receptionist asked straight out, Savannah wouldn't lie. But making a simple implication was another thing entirely.

He didn't ask. Instead, he turned away and picked up a telephone. Despite her best efforts, Savannah could catch only a word or two. She thought she heard him say something about Mr. Caine, and then her name, and the word *blonde*. Interesting, she thought. What did the color of her hair have to do with anything?

He put the telephone down, and she braced herself for questions. But the young man said, "Sixth floor. Take the elevator at the far end."

Savannah almost gasped in astonishment. Then she walked briskly to the elevator before the young man could change his mind. Of course, she reminded herself, getting past the receptionist hardly guaranteed she'd get into the executive offices; there'd no doubt be a couple of layers of secretaries to brave. But she'd already done better than she'd expected.

The sixth floor had no signs, no nameplates on doors, no receptionist, and no hint of the man she was looking for. Great, Savannah thought. I'll probably manage to give myself away just by asking where I'm supposed to go!

But there didn't seem to be anyone to ask, either. She had almost circled the balcony before she saw an office with an open door. Inside, a man sat on the corner of a desk with a telephone in his hand. It was not Dexter Caine—he was too young and too fair-haired—and Savannah hesitated for only an instant before walking on.

"Just a minute," the man murmured into the telephone. He put the receiver down on the desk blotter and came across to the door. "It took you long enough to get up here," he said. He sounded just a little peevish.

Savannah didn't see why he was complaining. In her opinion, the elevator had been unexpectedly fast for its vintage, but of course she had wandered around a bit before reaching his door. "Some directions would have helped. Have you ever considered putting signs up?'

"Not really. People who come here usually know where they're going."

Dandy, Savannah thought. Why don't you just open your mouth and stick your foot clear down your throat next time?

He smiled, and the irritable lines between his brows disappeared. "At any rate, let's forget about signs and get down to business. It's Friday, and we're all in a bit of a hurry, I'm sure."

Savannah shifted her bag slightly. "Now that you mention it—"

"Here, let me help." The man leaped forward and took the bag from her, drawing her into the office.

"Actually, I'm looking for Mr. Caine," she said cautiously.

"Of course. I'm Mr. Caine's personal assistant, Peter Powell. And your name is . . . I'm afraid I didn't write it down when the receptionist called up."

"Savannah Seabrooke."

"Ah, yes."

He looked thoughtful, as if the name had a familiar ring. Savannah wondered if he'd read the *Tribune* piece last year. Rather than give him a chance to think about it, she said firmly, "I'm sure Mr. Caine will want to see me himself."

"Oh, yes, I expect you're right."

Savannah almost choked. Could it really be as easy as that?

"In fact," he went on easily, "I've got a limo waiting for you downstairs."

But he couldn't have—the car couldn't possibly have been ordered for Savannah. Peter Powell had obviously mistaken her for someone else. But if she kept silent and played along....

Whoever Dexter Caine was expecting, he'd get a bit of a shock if Savannah turned up instead. A tinge of guilt tugged at her at the mere thought of taking advantage of this misunderstanding. No, she couldn't do that.

Though...why couldn't she? She wasn't likely to have a chance like this ever again. She could get into that car and be taken directly to Dexter Caine. And once there, all she needed was a couple of minutes. He'd have to say something to her, wouldn't he? If she turned up at his table at the fanciest restaurant in town, or at his box at Wrigley Field, or at his seats at the theater, he couldn't just toss her out without a word. And all she needed was one answer to one question....

What kind of reporter are you, Seabrooke? she asked herself. How can you even think of turning down this opportunity?

"Thanks," she said coolly. "That's very thoughtful of you." She reached for her bag.

"I'll walk down with you and carry that."

Her throat tightened. All she wanted was to get out of here as soon as possible, before Peter Powell recognized his error. "Don't bother. I'm used to carrying it. And I don't want to keep you from your telephone call."

"Oh—I'd forgotten that. If you're sure...." But Peter Powell was already reaching for the phone as Savannah picked up her tote bag.

The chauffeur had moved around to the street side of the car, and he looked Savannah over as she approached. "Excuse me," she said firmly. "I believe you're waiting for me. I'm Mr. Caine's guest." Then she held her breath.

Test number two, she thought. Would the chauffeur realize that she wasn't the passenger he was waiting for?

He snapped to attention and held the rear door for her. Savannah climbed in, trying her best to look as if she maneuvered in and out of a limousine every day, and he almost ran around to take his seat. A moment later the car nudged its way into rush-hour traffic.

And now what? Savannah thought. She eyed the two-way telephone built into the console in a corner of the limo. But she could hardly pick it up and ask the chauffeur where they were going.

It was quickly apparent they weren't headed anywhere in the Loop, or even in the city itself. That eliminated most of the fancy restaurants. And a good thing, too, Savannah thought. She hadn't considered before that her jeans wouldn't get her past the door of most of the city's elite dining spots. At least she wouldn't have to suffer the frustration of coming so close to Dexter Caine and missing out after all.

So where were they going? The limo turned smoothly onto the Kennedy Expressway, and Savannah drew a short, sharp breath. O'Hare? Surely they weren't headed for the airport!

They were; forty-five minutes later the limousine swooped off the expressway and past the main terminal—

Past it? Savannah thought in astonishment. She realized she was clutching the strap of her tote bag as if it were a security blanket, and loosened her grip.

The limousine drew up on an out-of-the-way bit of tarmac, where a gleaming blue-and-white airplane waited. Savannah's experience with aircraft was limited, but it didn't take an expert to know that this one was new, expensive, and very fast—it looked like a miniaturized version of the jetliners she was used to. She studied it warily while the chauffeur came around to open her door.

Actually, she decided, it wasn't such a bad turn of events. In the limited space and isolation of a small aircraft, she stood a pretty decent chance of getting something quotable out of Dexter Caine in the couple of minutes it would take him to react and throw her off the plane. Then she'd hike over to the main terminal and catch a shuttle back downtown. It would be dead easy—comparatively speaking.

A uniformed man appeared at the aircraft's door. "Good evening, miss," he said politely, and extended a hand to help Savannah climb the stairs.

The chauffeur still stood at attention beside the limousine door. Savannah glanced back at him and was touched when he raised two fingers to his cap in salute. She waved, feeling foolishly that she was losing her only friend, and took a deep breath before turning toward the cabin and her encounter with Dexter Caine.

The interior of the plane looked like a space-age living room, with low tables, built-in consoles, and wide plush seats that looked almost like easy chairs. There were only a few, though there was room for more.

And every seat was empty.

Savannah looked around wildly for a moment. He had to be somewhere, didn't he? Was there another cabin somewhere?

Behind her, the door closed with a soft click. She spun around to see the crewman indicating a seat. "If you'll just get comfortable and fasten your seat belt, miss, we'll be on our way momentarily."

"Mr.—" Her voice was harsh, and she had to stop to clear her throat. "What about Mr. Caine?"

The crewman's eyebrows rose slightly. "You'll be our only passenger this evening, miss."

"But—" She swallowed the half-formed protest. Better not say anything more till she'd had a chance to think. Not that a couple of minutes' delay was likely to do any good—if she had a week, she'd still be figuring out all the implications of this twist.

It hadn't occurred to her till this instant that Dexter Caine might not be in Chicago at all. The limousine that had prompted her to go into the building in the first place had been waiting for an unknown passenger, not him—why hadn't she remembered that sooner? And though the reactions of the receptionist and the personal assistant had led her to believe that their boss was nearby, that was no more than an assumption. Peter Powell had said only that he had a car waiting for her....

The hum of the engines grew a bit louder, and Savannah had to grab for a seat to steady herself as the plane suddenly began to move. "I think I'd better get off," she said. She felt as if her teeth were chattering.

The crewman was watching her warily. "If you're afraid of flying, miss, let me assure you that Captain Johnson is very skilled."

"Oh—no, I'm not afraid to fly. It's just that...." Her voice trailed off helplessly. Her brain felt absolutely blank.

"There are snacks and cold drinks in the refrigerator," the crewman said. "I'm afraid we're not really prepared for dinner, since we anticipated you'd arrive earlier."

That reminded Savannah that she was substituting for someone else, someone who had been expected to make this trip. The woman who had stood up Dexter Caine was causing trouble for a lot of people, that was sure.

Why wasn't that woman on this plane instead? And who was she? Not Cassie King, obviously—nearly everyone in North America knew her face. Besides, Peter Powell had accepted Savannah's name without question. That must mean the woman was a mystery to him, as well....

My head hurts, Savannah thought.

"We'll only be in the air for a few hours," the crewman went on, "so I don't think you'll find it too inconvenient."

"Where are we going?"

It was a stupid question, but it was out before Savannah could stop herself. She waited, breath held. The worst that could happen was that they'd throw her off the plane now, right on the runway.

But the crewman showed no surprise at a passenger who didn't know her destination. He was either used to such things, or so well trained that he was never at a loss. "Las Vegas, miss."

Vegas. Well, she supposed that made sense; Dexter Caine had business interests there. At least it wasn't Hong Kong, or Sydney, or New Delhi, or any of the many more exotic places where he also had business interests.

The plane was at the end of the runway, about to start its takeoff roll. That fact alone would have told Savannah something about its owner, if she'd been in any condition to think about it. O'Hare's delays were legendary, but it seemed the control tower had been waiting on this plane, not the reverse.

With a fatalistic sigh, Savannah dropped into a seat and pulled the belt tight.

The crewman seemed to relax. "If there's anything you need, miss, just press this bell." He pointed at a button on the bulkhead near her seat, and then passed through a narrow door into the cockpit.

Now I'm in for it, Savannah thought. Nothing like a quick side trip to Vegas.

If she managed to get Dexter Caine to talk to her, maybe Brian and the magazine would stand the cost of her flight home. Though considering Caine was getting Savannah instead of the woman—whoever she was—that he was waiting for, he probably wasn't going to be in a chatty mood.

Savannah settled back in her seat and nervously chewed her thumbnail all the way to Las Vegas.

The sun was setting when the plane landed; Savannah tried to enjoy the spectacle of the desert aflame with the last rays of daylight. A limousine—white this time—was waiting in an out-of-the-way corner far from the terminal, with another uniformed chauffeur beside it.

Without a word he ushered her into the car. Savannah held her breath till she realized she was alone, and then couldn't quite make up her mind whether to be anxious or relieved that Dexter Caine still hadn't shown up. At least the limousine would have been a quiet, private place to have a chat—and she wouldn't have had to find her way back to the airport.

She'd spent a good deal of the flight mentally reviewing what she knew about Dexter Caine, so she wasn't surprised when the limousine drew up in front of one of Las Vegas's older hotel-casino combinations, not one of the new and glitzy theme resorts.

He'd come into possession of this property only recently, and there had been some speculation about precisely how and why he'd ended up owning it. A hotel was one thing, but Savannah agreed that a casino seemed an odd thing for a man like Dexter Caine to want. He was the sort who preferred gambling on other things besides cards and dice and slot machines.

I'll keep that for my second question, Savannah thought. Always assuming she was allowed time for more than one.

At the hotel's side entrance, the chauffeur handed her over to the bell captain, who whisked her straight through the lobby and up the freight elevator, without even a glimpse of the casino area or the main lobby. "This is standard procedure," he apologized as he unlocked the door of a penthouse suite. "Mr. Caine prefers his privacy."

Savannah's eyes widened in appreciation. She had never seen such an incredible array of Art Deco furnishings outside of a museum, but the way it was arranged made the rooms comfortable and welcoming—almost cozy—not at all like the usual hotel room.

A fire burned brightly in a classically simple polished-marble fireplace. Nearby, a couple of couches were arranged at an angle to provide the best view of the blaze. Wall sconces cast a welcoming glow. On a low table was a fruit basket and a dish of chocolate truffles. Off to one side of the big room was a starkly simple dining area; beyond it she could see the corner of an all-white kitchen.

A white-haired man in a dark suit came out of the kitchen. "Thank you, John," he said, and bowed slightly to Savannah. "Good evening, miss. I'm Robinson, the butler."

This was obviously how the other half lived—a suite with its own butler. Savannah had never in her life encountered such a person, and she hadn't the vaguest idea how to proceed. She took comfort in the fact that she *did* know how to treat the bell captain; she fumbled in the side pocket of her tote bag for her wallet, but by the time she found it, he had silently vanished and her tip stayed folded in her fingers.

Obviously a gaffe, she thought. The butler looked even more wooden, but at least he didn't comment.

"If you'd like to freshen up, Miss..."

"Seabrooke," Savannah supplied warily, and relaxed a little when he merely nodded. So Robinson didn't know who the mystery guest was, either, she concluded.

Savannah was beginning to feel extremely curious about that woman. "Is Mr. Caine in the hotel?"

Robinson's tone was stiflingly flat. "I really couldn't say, miss."

Which meant exactly nothing, Savannah deduced. "I'd love to freshen up," she said. She couldn't do much, of course—she had only the bits of makeup that she carried in the side pocket of her tote bag. But at least she could hide for a while from the butler's all-seeing eyes.

She let him carry her tote bag to a bedroom at the far end of the suite. Then she firmly closed the door behind him and took a deep breath of relief.

The room was huge, with a king-size bed covered by a satin comforter the color of polished pewter. French doors led onto a spacious balcony. Near the windows was a small square table and two straight-backed chairs. It was nice enough, but much less welcoming than the living room.

The clock on the bedside table said it was only eight, but Savannah's body was still on Chicago time, and she was starting to feel a bit woozy from exhaustion and stress. She looked around for a comfortable chair, but there wasn't one, so she sagged onto the end of the bed. "What kind of hotel is this anyway?" she muttered. "A butler, for heaven's sake—but no easy chair in the bedroom!" The sound of her own voice made her feel a bit better, but the apprehension at the pit of her stomach remained. What had she gotten herself into? How was she going to get out? And where the devil was Dexter Caine?

Much later, Savannah remembered taking her boots off, because it had felt so good to flex her toes. And she vaguely recalled that round about midnight she'd pulled the pillows into a more comfortable position and curled up to wait for Dexter Caine. It was no wonder that she'd dozed off; her eyelids had been so heavy it would have taken props to keep them open.

So when the dream started, she had no trouble figuring out what was happening to her. She'd had a few wildly romantic—even erotic—dreams in her time. They were most likely to occur when she was stressed and short of sleep, and that description certainly fit her current state. In fact, her stress level probably explained why this particular dream was turning into a doozy.

And considering that she'd had Dexter Caine on her mind when she dozed off, it was no wonder that he featured in her dreams, as well.

Still, she'd never experienced anything so realistic. She'd never been kissed so expertly before, or held so warmly close, or...

Deep in her brain a voice of warning sounded. This isn't *realistic,* it said. This is *real.*

CHAPTER TWO

OPENING her eyes required an effort of will, and Savannah almost gave up the task before she'd accomplished it. It was far easier to believe that she was asleep after all and only dreaming that she was awake, as happened sometimes.

She still thought it was odd, though; she'd never had such a very graphic dream before. Of course, imagination was an amazing thing. Savannah could actually feel a hand moving slowly from the small of her back up her spine. She could feel the pressure of a body warm and taut against hers. She could feel the slight scrape of a stubbly beard against the sensitive skin of her throat....

Now that was very strange, she thought. She'd never dreamed up an unshaven hero before.

Her eyes popped open and widened in shock. Directly above her was a face the size of a billboard. She blinked and looked again.

It took her a moment to focus and realize that the face wasn't actually as large as it first appeared. It—*he*—was just so close to her that he'd seemed larger than life, and the dim glow of the moon, filtering through the sheer curtains and providing the only light in the room, increased the effect. He was so close, in fact, that his breath stirred her eyelashes. From chest to toes she was pressed against him so tightly that the hairs on his chest threatened to leave permanent dents in her body.

He wasn't kissing her anymore, though the tingle in her lips warned that she hadn't been dreaming that particular caress, any more than she had imagined the way his hands were wandering up her spine. He was, however,

24

nuzzling her temple, his mouth warm against the tender skin.

"What are you doing?" Instead of the firm, assertive, self-assured note she'd been trying for, Savannah's voice sounded small and wavery.

"What am *I* doing?" He drew back a couple of inches. "I came in here, found you asleep, and started to shake you awake. The next thing I know I'm flat on the bed beside you, held captive and being kissed within an inch of my life. It's not that I'm complaining, you understand, but nevertheless—"

Savannah gasped. "I didn't!"

"Oh, but you did. As a matter of fact, you still *are.* I'm not the one who's holding you down."

Savannah lifted her head a little. He was right; she was lying half on top of him, with one of her legs draped over both of his, and she was clutching him with both arms. Or, as she preferred to think of the situation, she had simply reached out in her sleep to hold on to the nearest solid object in order to keep her balance.

He was definitely solid. His ribs were hard, his muscles firm. There didn't seem to be a spare ounce on him.

She realized that her hands were exploring under his shirt, and abruptly she let go and rolled away, putting one hand up to cover her eyes. Maybe if she didn't look at him she wouldn't feel quite so embarrassed.

"Well, I suppose all good things must come to an end." He turned on the bedside lamp and settled back comfortably, propping himself on one elbow, to study her. "Who are you anyway?"

Savannah was taken aback by the cool, calm question. He'd been expecting another woman entirely. Shouldn't he be angry? Concerned? Upset? Instead, he sounded mildly curious—and that was all.

She wondered when he'd realized that she wasn't the woman he'd been expecting to be waiting for him here. Had the moonlight shown him her face when he first came in? Surely not, or he wouldn't have greeted her so amorously—Savannah refused to believe his contention that *she'd* started that little wrestling match. But surely, once he'd touched her, he'd have quickly recognized from the feel of her body that she was different....

Savannah wondered how the woman he'd been expecting to find would have reacted to his greeting. She turned her head to stare at him, and decided with her first really good look at Dexter Caine that the question didn't require a lot of imagination to answer.

Savannah would have known him anywhere. The light from the bedside lamp slanted across his face and cut it into angles, showing off the strong lines of a classic profile. The facial structure, the aristocratic set of his ears, the big dark eyes—those features were apparent in even the worst photos of Dexter Caine. But as for the rest....

She hadn't realized from the tabloid photographs—which usually showed him scowling at the camera—that he was so extraordinarily good-looking. She hadn't known before that his eyes weren't black, but a deep mellow brown. She'd had no idea he was so big—his body stretched most of the length of the bed, and his shoulders seemed incredibly broad. She'd never even seen him pictured without a jacket—much less with his shirt unbuttoned to show off the lean muscles that rippled in his chest. And she'd never seen his hair drooping casually over his forehead as it was this moment as he leaned over her....

Of course, she'd never seen a picture of him lying down, either. From this angle he appeared—

Savannah realized abruptly that continuing to lie on the bed could be interpreted as an invitation, so she sat up, clutching one of the pillows to her chest as if it were an armor-plated shield.

He was studying her with painful intensity, and she had to look away. She noted that his evening coat and bow tie had been draped over the back of one of the chairs. She supposed she should be glad he'd stopped at that before coming to greet.... Who was the woman who should have been here instead of her? It was terribly frustrating not to know anything about her.

"Is there some reason I shouldn't know who you are?" he said.

She'd forgotten that he'd asked. She shook her head and almost stammered her name.

"Savannah Seabrooke," he repeated. His voice turned the syllables into a caress. "Nice." The way he said it—combined with the appraising way he looked at her—sent a wave of warm color over Savannah's face.

This was getting out of hand. The sooner she made him realize that she wasn't here to be a plaything, the better. "I don't know who you were expecting to be here when you came in, Mr. Caine, but—"

"Oh, call me Dexter. I imagine you'll do just fine instead."

"Look, I don't know what you think I'm here for, but—"

"Didn't they tell you anything at all?" He sat up. "Damn. That's a nuisance."

Savannah, uneasy at any movement that brought him closer, shifted nervously toward the foot of the bed. "But you've had your revenge now, okay?"

His eyebrows lifted. They were dark and heavy, and suddenly he looked almost threatening. "Revenge?"

"For me not being the person you expected."

"I told you I don't mind the switch."

She was startled. "You really don't?"

"Of course not."

"But—" Before she could consider whether the question was wise, she asked, "Who on earth were you expecting, then? Some kind of expensive lady of pleasure?"

His eyes glinted a little. "Oh, no."

Savannah breathed a little easier.

He added, "Not *expensive,* exactly. After all, they do say all women are pretty much alike in the dark." He slid toward her, and the soft whisper of his body shifting against the satin comforter sent icicles down Savannah's spine.

"It's not dark in here," she managed.

Dexter Caine shrugged. "We can soon fix that. Though after the demonstration you gave me a few minutes ago, I'm not so sure I believe that old proverb anymore anyway." He slid across the bed toward her.

Savannah was too frozen to move. But he simply turned the clock on the bedside table till he could see the time. Savannah saw it, too; it was just a little past three o'clock.

Suddenly his voice was very brisk. "This is great fun, but let's talk it over in the morning, all right? It's been a beastly long day, I'm exhausted, and I really am not in the mood to explain everything tonight. I'd have thought that was the agency's job anyway."

What agency? Savannah decided this wasn't the prudent moment to ask. "Fine. See you in the morning."

Dexter Caine gave her a half smile and slid back across the bed till he could reach the lamp he'd turned on. He snapped it off, pulled a pillow into position, and stretched out with a sigh.

Savannah's eyes widened in shock. "You're not staying here!"

He didn't move. "Why not? It's my bedroom."

And the butler had brought her in here? Who *had* he been expecting? What had she gotten herself into? And how was she going to get out?

Within two minutes Dexter Caine was breathing evenly and quietly, obviously sound asleep. Savannah sat at the end of the bed and considered her options. In her tote bag she had twenty dollars in cash and a credit card that was charged almost to the limit; there was no way she could afford a room in this hotel tonight and still buy a ticket back to Chicago tomorrow.

Besides, if she left the suite she'd never get back in, and she still hadn't accomplished what she'd set out to do—she hadn't managed to get anything quotable from Dexter Caine.

It wasn't surprising, she reassured herself, that in the confusion she'd forgotten all about her original purpose. Waking up in the man's arms would tend to demolish any woman's self-control.

There was the couch in the suite's living room, of course, but if she moved out there, the butler might hear, and she could end up out in the cold in the middle of the night.

No, her only option was to stay put and keep a close eye on Dexter Caine. First thing in the morning, she'd introduce herself—it was only ethical, after all, to let him know he was talking to a reporter before she started asking too many questions—and then she'd worry about how to get home.

She gathered up the extra pillows, moving slowly and cautiously so as not to disturb him, and built a wall down the middle of the big bed. Then she settled back on her side, her back propped against the headboard, to wait for morning.

She wouldn't go to sleep, of course. Considering what had happened last time, it wouldn't be prudent.

It wasn't an erotic dream this time, just a pleasant fantasy of floating on a cloud that rocked her like a baby. Savannah didn't want to let go of it, and she shook her head and buried her face in the cloud. But it wasn't as soft as she'd expected, and it scratched her face. And it rumbled....

No, that sound was a muffled laugh. "Wake up, sweetheart," a voice murmured into her ear. "Robinson's going to be coming in any minute."

She opened her eyes. She was cradled in his arms, with her face pressed against his chest, and the rocking sensation she'd felt was his breathing. Rattled, she tried desperately to gather the remaining shreds of her dignity. "I must have drifted off for a moment," she said.

"Something like that," Dexter Caine said agreeably.

No wonder she'd felt wrapped in a cloud—she was snuggled up squarely in the center of the bed, with the pillows under and around her in a state of disarray. As the desert chill had crept into the room through the night, she had unconsciously sought warmth, and she'd found it in Dexter Caine's body. If she'd been embarrassed last night at the way she'd been wrapped around him, this morning she was mortified by the position she found herself in.

"Of course, I'm not complaining," he went on. The way his voice vibrated deep in his chest tickled Savannah's cheek.

A knock sounded from the hall. "It's all right, Robinson," Dexter called, and the butler came in before Savannah could even protest.

She would have liked to dive under the comforter. On the other hand, she supposed that would only make things look worse.

Swift-footed, Robinson moved silently across the room to open the sheer curtains and let the morning sun stream across the carpet. He did not seem to notice the couple on the bed.

Dexter stretched, releasing his hold on Savannah. "Good morning, Robinson."

"Good morning, sir. It promises to be a very pleasant day."

I think I'll just pretend to be invisible, Savannah decided.

Dexter gave her a lazy grin. "By the way, you owe Robinson an apology, my dear."

Savannah could feel heat surging to her cheeks. "Why?" Too late, she decided she didn't want to know.

"I forgot to tell you he was very concerned last night. He was still hovering outside this door when I got here, waiting for you to come out so he could turn the bed down. He takes his duties very seriously, you see."

"Mr. Caine exaggerates, miss," the butler said woodenly. "Breakfast in fifteen minutes, sir?"

"That'll be fine, Robinson. Anything particular you'd like, darling?"

"No, thanks," Savannah muttered, and added with pure pique, "Robinson may not care, but I'd appreciate it if you'd try to remember my name." Not that it mattered, of course; she wouldn't be around long.

"Whatever makes you think I've forgotten it, Savannah?" Dexter relaxed against a pile of pillows and looked at her with one eyebrow quirked inquiringly. Even half-dressed, his remaining clothes rumpled, he managed to look perfectly assured and in command of the situation. He'd obviously forgotten all about the butler.

Savannah couldn't; she watched over Dexter's shoulder as Robinson gathered up the jacket and tie from the chair back. Only after he'd left the room as quietly as he'd come in did she slide off the bed. There was no mirror in the bedroom, but she could see enough of her reflection in the shiny silver base of the bedside lamp to know that she looked decidedly the worse for wear.

Fifteen minutes later, when she reached the dining table, she didn't feel a whole lot better. A hot shower had restored her, but getting back into her crumpled jeans, wrinkled shirt, and creased blazer hadn't improved her mood or her self-confidence. What she wouldn't give right now for a travel iron!

Dexter Caine, on the other hand, looked as if he'd just stepped out of his tailor's shop. His gray suit was immaculate, his shirt brilliantly white, and his dark red tie perfectly knotted. He rose to hold her chair.

"Robinson's making omelets," he said. "I hope you like them?"

"Sounds wonderful. I'm starving."

"Well, it's your own fault. He told me you refused dinner."

Last night, she'd felt a little squeamish about eating the man's food when she was there under false pretenses. This morning, she was hungry enough to feel no such qualms.

Robinson set a platter-size omelet before her, and Savannah buttered a slice of toast and feasted on the glorious aroma for a full minute before she cut into the golden half circle and savored the first rich bite.

Dexter sampled his own breakfast. "I want to apologize for what happened last night, Savannah."

She looked at him warily. The last thing she would have expected from Dexter Caine was anything resembling an apology.

"I was very tired," he went on, "and you did greet me as if I'd just come home from the Crusades—but that's no excuse for letting my sense of humor get out of hand. Instead of teasing you, I should have told you what this is all about. As it is, I feel as if I've brought you here under false pretenses."

Savannah almost choked on a bite of toast. *That's your cue*, she told herself. After what he'd just told her, it should have been easy to smile and say, *Oh, that's all right. And while we're on the subject, I've got some false pretenses of my own to confess.* But the words stuck in her throat like wallpaper paste.

"Of course," Dexter went on, "even the agency didn't know much about what I want—just the bare bones of the job. In a situation like this, obviously, I didn't want the details too widely known. But I'm sure you'll be able to carry it off with—"

Robinson appeared at his elbow with the coffeepot. "Sir, Mr. Powell is downstairs, and he insists on seeing you immediately."

Savannah could feel the blood draining from her face. And though she wasn't looking directly at Dexter just then, she knew he was watching her, and she could sense the interest in his gaze.

"What's he doing here? He's supposed to be in Chicago, taking care of...." From the corner of her eye, she could see the frown lines between his brows. "Have him come up, Robinson."

Savannah bit her lip and looked down at the piece of toast she'd been unconsciously shredding.

"Savannah." Dexter's voice was implacable, and she looked up at him against her will. "Do you know anything about this?"

There wasn't time for an answer, even if she'd had some glib explanation ready, for Peter Powell came in just then; he must not have waited downstairs for the command.

Peter paused at the edge of the geometric rug that defined the dining area and stared at Savannah. "So you're here, then."

He looked different than he had just yesterday, Savannah thought—as if he'd lost ten pounds, a week's sleep, and half his color. Of course, next to Dexter's tan and his size, most men would look pale and rather weak....

Don't get distracted, she warned herself. This could be a dangerous situation.

"Obviously she's here," Dexter said. "What about it? Didn't you send her?"

Peter Powell shifted from one foot to the other. "Well—yes."

"Then what's the problem?"

"She's an imposter, Mr. Caine. The agency didn't send her."

"Didn't you check her out?" Dexter's voice was gentle.

The assistant's Adam's apple bobbed.

Dexter sighed. "Sit down, Peter. Have a cup of coffee and take it from the top."

Peter scrambled into the chair across from Savannah's. He didn't look at her. "Well, it was late," he began. "I'd been waiting all afternoon for the woman the agency was sending, and so when the receptionist called up and told me she was there—"

"You took his word for it?"

"Well, it was obvious, I thought. She looked enough like the description you'd given me—"

"What description?" Savannah said. Then she remembered the receptionist saying something about a blonde while she waited in the lobby. She hadn't caught the rest, but she remembered wondering why it mattered what color her hair was. "So you like blondes, Mr. Caine?" she murmured.

"Now and then," Dexter said. "As it happens, though, I had a specific person in mind this time."

"I thought you said it didn't matter!"

"It wasn't critical. I just thought Muffy would—"

"Muffy?" Savannah almost howled. "The woman you were expecting last night answers to *Muffy*?"

Dexter glared at her. If looks could burn, she'd have been a cinder.

"So anyway," Peter went on, "I thought she was just a substitute. You did say to tell the agency that if Muffy wasn't available, someone else would do, Mr. Caine. Besides, she was carrying an overnight bag, and she seemed to know what she was doing."

"Now that much I can believe," Dexter murmured. "You're a very talented little actress, I'd say, Savannah. What inspired you to come on this gig anyway?"

Savannah shrugged. "Curiosity." It was almost the truth after all.

Dexter didn't comment, but the look he gave her made it clear he found the answer less than adequate. "So what happened, Peter?"

"I put her in the limo. Then I finished up my work and went home. I was at a party last night when the receptionist called and said there was another woman there and she insisted on seeing me, so I went over to find out what she wanted—"

"During the party?" Dexter murmured. "What selfless devotion, Peter."

Peter's jaw worked for a moment before he confessed, "I waited till after the party. When I found out the agency had sent her—they'd made a mistake and told her the wrong address, so she'd been trying to find me for hours—well, I knew this woman wasn't what she'd said she was." He jabbed a finger in Savannah's direction.

"I didn't say anything," Savannah pointed out. "You assumed a lot."

Peter turned back to Dexter. "I tried to call you right away, but you weren't in the hotel. I didn't figure you'd want me to spill the details to anyone else, even to Robinson—"

"You've got that much right."

"So I got the first flight I could and came straight out."

Dexter leaned back in his chair, his coffee cup balanced in the palm of his hand. "What did you do with the other woman, Peter?"

"Her name's Martha. She's downstairs."

"Why?"

"Why?" Peter's voice rose as if he didn't quite believe what he was hearing. "Because I knew you wouldn't want this one, once you found out she's an imposter."

Savannah braced herself for the rest, but Peter stopped there. Maybe that meant he still didn't know the worst of it, she thought. Knowing the agency hadn't sent her didn't mean Peter Powell had discovered she was a reporter. Now that was an implication worth thinking through...if she'd only had time.

Dexter Caine reached for the coffeepot Robinson had left and refilled his cup. "Have you told Martha about the job?"

Peter shook his head. "Of course not. I said you wanted to talk to her yourself, and I hinted about some modeling work. That's all."

Savannah thought, A model? What on earth did Dexter Caine want with a model?

"Sometimes, Peter," Dexter mused, "you show a glimmer—just a glimmer—of potential."

"Thank you, sir." There was a thread of relief in Peter's voice.

"Since Martha's still in the dark," Dexter went on, "there's no harm done. You can just take her back to Chicago with you. Tell her the job fell through, apologize profusely, and pay her standard modeling rates for her time. Then call the talent agency and tell them we don't need their services any longer, and that'll be the end of it."

"But...what are you going to do, sir? Give up the whole idea?"

"Oh, no. Savannah will do just fine. I've been telling her about the job—"

"You didn't!" Peter howled. "About Cassie King and the stories she's making up and *everything*? Mr. Caine—"

That was all the confirmation she needed, Savannah thought. She'd hit the jackpot; her instincts had been right, and she could go back to Brian now with her story complete.

Of course, she'd bent the ethics a bit by not telling Dexter she was a reporter before she asked her questions. On the other hand, she hadn't really asked. A reporter wasn't obligated to identify herself if all she was doing was eavesdropping, was she? And in a sense. . . .

Another foggy idea was tugging at the corners of her mind. Something clicked in Savannah's brain like the meshing of gears, and suddenly she knew why Dexter Caine had hired a Chicago blonde and brought her to Vegas. It was an outlandish scheme, an audacious plot— but it made sense, and it was an intrigue worthy of Dexter Caine.

"It was an actress you needed, wasn't it?" she said quietly. "Not a model. You wanted her to play a part and convince the world that no matter what Cassie King says, you're not going to marry her. That way you can discredit Cassie's stories and make fools of the media and still not violate your privacy. Right?"

There was a flicker of respect in Dexter's eyes. "Close enough."

"You're going to cause yourself a lot of trouble, you know. Once the media has a reason to wonder about you—"

Dexter Caine wasn't listening. He turned to Peter. "Why shouldn't Savannah help out? She's smart and quick and convincing, that's clear—and she already knows what's going on. Why take someone else into the secret when she'll do just fine?"

Savannah said, "That's all very flattering, but—"

Peter interrupted. "But, sir, she's . . . she's not just an imposter. She's a reporter."

She'd underestimated him after all, Savannah realized. He'd simply been trying to the bitter end to protect himself by keeping the worst news from his boss, hoping it would never have to come out.

She sneaked a look at Dexter's face, which looked as if it had been cast in steel. "Are you?" he said coolly.

She nodded. "Peter doesn't need to make it sound like a criminal activity, though."

Peter added helpfully, "She's the one who did the feature on you last year in the *Chicago Tribune*."

"That hatchet job?" Dexter's eyes were suddenly furnace hot.

"It wasn't!" Savannah protested. "It was a very flattering piece!"

"Opinions differ. You said you came out of curiosity," he mused. "I wonder why it didn't occur to me to ask how you found out what was going on? Do you have a spy in the talent agency?"

"Of course not. I just happened into your building at the right moment, and it was obvious something interesting was going on, so I played along. I wanted to ask you some questions about your relationship with Cassie King. As a matter of fact, there are still some things I'd like to know. So, as long as we're talking about it now—"

Dexter's voice cracked like a whip. "This entire conversation is off the record!"

"You can't take a discussion off the record after it happens," Savannah explained patiently. "That has to be agreed on beforehand."

"How could it be agreed on when you never identified yourself?"

"You hardly gave me a chance. Sorry, Mr. Caine, but what's happened here this morning *is* on the record."

"Oh?" His voice suddenly had a silky note that was somehow even more terrifying than the whiplash had been. "You're quite firm about that?"

Savannah nodded, trying her best to keep her chin from wobbling. There wasn't anything to be afraid of, was there? She was right, and he couldn't change the facts. "Absolutely. I'm free to write about everything I heard and saw here."

Dexter didn't answer. There was a tight little line at each corner of his mouth. Savannah wondered if that was how he looked on the rare occasions when he was bested in a business deal.

"Peter," he said gently, "remember what I said a few minutes ago about your having occasional glimmers of potential? This has not been one of those times. You're fired."

Savannah said quickly, "That's really not fair, Mr. Caine."

"Oh? Does that mean you're taking all the blame for this little episode? Did you enchant Peter, or merely seduce him?"

"Of course I'm not taking all the blame. But don't you think you're being a little too hasty? I don't know how long Peter's worked for you, but he's obviously devoted, and—"

Dexter eyed her in very much the same way he'd observe a poisonous snake loose on his breakfast table. But he said agreeably, "Perhaps you're right. I might be acting too hastily. Peter, pick up the woman downstairs and take her back to Chicago. *Then* you're fired."

Peter gulped and hung his head. "Yes, Mr. Caine."

"Wait a minute," Savannah said. "Don't you need her? Or are you canceling the scheme after all?"

Dexter smiled. There was no humor in the expression. "Why would I need her? I have you." He waved Peter out of the room.

Savannah laughed. "Oh, come on. You don't want me."

"That's beside the point, don't you think? I can't let you go. You know too much about this."

She could feel her heartbeat pounding in her ears. She told herself it was silly to be afraid, but it didn't help much. "What if I promise not to tell?"

"And I'm supposed to believe you? How convenient that would be—for you. You said just a couple of minutes ago that you planned to write it all."

"No, I didn't." She shrank just a bit under his dark, disbelieving gaze, and muttered, "Not exactly."

"And you've probably got your fingers crossed behind your back, too. No, you're staying where I can keep an eye on you."

Savannah put her chin up and struck back. "How do I know you didn't do this on purpose? Maybe Peter recognized my name as soon as he heard it yesterday, so you told him to lure me onto the plane and you brought me out here to discredit me. It could have been you he was talking to—"

Even before Dexter started laughing, she realized how silly the whole line of reasoning sounded.

"You said yourself that I don't want you," Dexter pointed out. "But now that I'm stuck with you, I might as well proceed with my plan—with you in the starring role."

"Oh, really? What if I don't want to play along?"

"You don't have a choice."

"You can't hold me captive here. It's—" She groped for some legal-sounding term. "It's felonious imprisonment."

"Actually," Dexter mused, "I'd prefer to call it a job opportunity. The conditions of employment might be somewhat unusual, but I think you'll agree that the benefits more than make up for—"

"This is kidnapping!"

"And what you tried to pull off is fraud." His voice was level, but no less threatening for its calmness.

Savannah bit her lip and wondered if he was right. She suspected he might be, but she'd rather go down fighting than surrender. "No, it's not. I didn't lie to anybody about who I am. I didn't even use an assumed name. I just didn't go into detail."

He didn't bother to answer, just stared at her as if he couldn't believe what he was hearing.

"I'll pay you back for the flight and everything," she offered. Despite her best efforts, her voice quavered a little.

"You certainly will." He was implacable. "We'll start this evening with a fleeting appearance in the casino downstairs—just enough to arouse a little curiosity." He pushed his chair back and rose.

"You're being very shortsighted," Savannah pointed out. "If you don't let me go now, I could do what you ask and then write about it later, with all the gory details. And you'll be a laughingstock."

He grinned down at her, his good humor restored. "I wouldn't be the only one. Try it, and I'll announce that you're a disappointed former lover who wants revenge because I dumped you. I think I'd actually enjoy making an exception to my rule about talking to the press in that case. And especially when they've got Cassie as a precedent, who do you think they'll believe?"

She could see him doing it, too, and wouldn't that be a juicy tidbit? Nobody would ever believe her side of it if Dexter Caine broke his self-imposed silence to issue a denial. Even the magazines that might pay for her story, just for the titillating details, would never be quite sure she was telling the truth.

And her career would be destroyed. A reporter who lost her credibility wasn't exactly a hot property.

She didn't have a lot of choices left, she realized. But maybe she could still salvage something from this disaster if she was fast enough. "All right. I'll stay, and I'll give this performance everything I've got."

"Somehow I thought you'd be agreeable in the end."

Savannah hadn't paused. "If I can write your authorized biography. The whole inside story of your life."

He braced both hands on the table and stared at her. "You have the unmitigated gall to negotiate with me? You'll play this part, and you'll damned well be convincing, or I'll charge you with trespassing, fraud and theft.''

"That's vile! I didn't do those things." At least not all of them; she'd have to admit to being guilty of trespassing, and possibly fraud. "What am I supposed to have stolen?''

"Do you really believe it matters? I'll think of something.''

All he'd have to do was slip a few trinkets into her bag, Savannah knew. Even the knife and fork she'd used to eat her omelet would be enough to get charges filed; they were sterling silver, and her fingerprints were all over the handles.

He leaned over her chair, hands firm on her shoulders. ''It's funny you should say what you did last night about my getting my revenge because you weren't the person I was expecting," he mused.

"So what's funny about that?''

He smiled grimly. "Remember this, Savannah—you haven't seen revenge yet. But believe me, you're going to.''

CHAPTER THREE

DEXTER CAINE strode off toward the bedroom, but Savannah could still feel the warm pressure of his hands resting on her shoulders long after he'd vanished. She stayed at the table, sitting up very straight.

What she longed to do was fling herself down flat somewhere and shed a few tears—but she was determined not to do that. In this particular case, she suspected that tears would get her nothing but puffy eyes and another sarcastic comment from Dexter Caine. And even if she could convince him she was sincere—which she didn't think was possible—she wasn't about to give him the satisfaction of seeing her cry.

A few minutes later, Robinson appeared, as silent-footed as ever, and began to clear the table. "Shall I take your plate away, miss?"

Savannah glanced at the omelet that had looked so good half an hour ago. "Please do. I don't think I can manage another bite. But if there's more coffee—"

"I'll make another pot immediately, miss." He left the room before she could tell him it didn't matter, she'd really only wanted something to occupy her hands.

It seemed no time at all before Robinson returned with the coffee and a fresh cup and saucer. He filled the cup and cleared his throat. "I understand you're to be with us for a while, Miss Seabrooke."

Savannah could catch nothing in his tone except polite respect. That surprised her, till she remembered Peter Powell saying something about Robinson not being included in the select few who knew the details of Dexter Caine's plan.

Well, that was just too bad, she thought. She'd agreed to put on a public performance because she didn't have any other choice, but Dexter hadn't said anything about having to convince the butler. Robinson had probably drawn his own conclusions anyway—he couldn't have escaped hearing that quarrel.

She let a wry note creep into her voice. "You understand correctly. How long, right now, is anybody's guess."

He bowed acknowledgment. "Is there anything that would make your stay more comfortable?"

A small dose of food poisoning for your boss, she almost said. But there wasn't any point in dragging Robinson into the middle of this. "Yes, there is. My own bedroom. I'm quite fond of my privacy, you see."

She was amazed to see Robinson turn ever so slightly pink. "Pardon me, miss. That *is* your bedroom."

She winced. He must think it had been at her invitation that Dexter Caine had spent the night with her. Though what he'd made of the fact that they'd both slept in their clothes was anybody's guess.

Savannah knew that people who were used to having servants around didn't generally care what they saw or thought. For instance, Dexter certainly hadn't let it bother him this morning when Robinson popped in to open the curtains. But she didn't fit comfortably in that level of society, and she'd rather not have the butler thinking there was hanky-panky going on.

"Oh, really?" she drawled. "Last night your precious Mr. Caine told me it was his."

Robinson almost stammered. "Well, he may have meant, in the sense that the whole suite is his—indeed the whole hotel—that one could make the case...."

"Don't bother trying to rescue him, Robinson. He probably doesn't need help. Your Mr. Caine is a charmer with words, isn't he?" Savannah's voice held an ironic edge. "How about getting me a good lock? And while

we're at it, I'd love a comfortable chair and a decent
reading light. I don't expect to come out of that room
very often."

Robinson's wooden look was back in place. "Yes,
miss."

"And I'm a news junkie, so I'd really love a paper in
the mornings."

"Any particular city or edition, miss, or would you
prefer a selection?"

Savannah stared at him in disbelief for a moment, and
then remembered the coffee. She wasn't used to such
instantaneous reactions to her wishes; she'd better remember to think things through before expressing a
desire. Though it would be interesting, she thought, to
see Dexter's reaction if he woke up tomorrow to an entire
newsstand in his living room.

"Whatever's easiest, Robinson. And one will do just
fine." She caught a glimpse of Dexter crossing the living
room toward the suite's main door, and she twisted
around in her chair and waved a hand like a schoolgirl
who needed permission to get up. "Warden?" she called.
"Oh, Warden!"

Dexter came across the room and stopped, pushing
his jacket back to put his hands on his hips. "You're
not in prison, Savannah. Not yet, at any rate." A jerk
of his head dismissed Robinson, who promptly vanished
into the kitchen, leaving his loaded tray behind.

Savannah smiled sweetly. "You'll have to pardon me
for getting confused. I'm so far out of my depth in this
situation, you see."

"You amaze me. Do you expect me to believe you've
never pulled a shady deal before? Or is it simply that no
one ever caught you red-handed?"

Savannah decided to ignore that one. "Might your
prisoner... oh, sorry. Might your humble guest be per-
mitted to hunt up a discount store to buy some little

luxuries? You know the sort of thing, I'm sure. A tooth-brush, some undies—''

He looked her over once more, and she was sure he noted the crumpled collar of her tailored blouse and every wrinkle in her blazer. "What do you have in that bag of yours?"

"Only my laptop computer and a few materials I'm sure you'd find subversive, like files on articles I'm writing. You see, when I left home yesterday, I didn't intend to be gone for— How long do you expect this to take anyway?"

He smiled a little. "Oh, you can just tell your boss you're taking an extended vacation." There was no mis-taking the flash of satisfaction in his eyes as he realized he was probably costing her a job, too.

Savannah saw no reason to disillusion him; this par-ticular petty outcropping of his revenge wasn't going to cost her anything, and allowing him this pleasure might keep him from thinking up something worse. "Thanks a lot," she grumbled.

"My pleasure. You're right about one thing, by the way."

She looked up at him in utter disbelief. "You're kidding. We actually agree on something? Let me make a note of this in my pocket calendar. What is it?"

"I shouldn't have fired Peter. It would have been proper penance for him to have to take you shopping."

"You know," she said thoughtfully, "maybe you should consider what happens if he talks."

"He won't."

"How can you be so certain? You can't have paid him that well. Besides, purchased loyalty generally lasts only till the final check's cashed."

"You sound as if that's a personal philosophy, Savannah. Do you have a lot of experience with pur-chased loyalty? Why do you want Peter back anyway?"

"I don't, particularly. I just think—"

"Do you believe he might be useful to you? Grateful, perhaps, because you salvaged his job?"

"Not at all. I just don't want to be the one who gets blamed if a story shows up somewhere because he calls up a reporter for a chat."

"I doubt it's Peter I'll have to worry about. You're very smooth, aren't you?"

"Obviously not smooth enough, or I wouldn't be here. So what am I supposed to do for clothes? Now that I think about it, if you want me to be convincing tonight in the casino, I'm going to need something other than jeans. What would you like me to wear? Flame red taffeta with a neckline down to here?" She pointed at her navel.

Dexter didn't answer. "Robinson!"

"Oh, dandy," Savannah muttered. "Don't you think he has enough to do already?"

"Certainly he does. Why do you ask?"

"I thought you were going to send him along to guard me."

"Oh, no. Robinson's a wonder, but I doubt he'd be up to that job." The butler appeared in the kitchen door, a towel wrapped around his waist, and Dexter said, "I'm taking Miss Seabrooke shopping. Call the office downstairs and tell my secretary to cancel all my appointments this morning, because I've been unavoidably detained."

"Terrific," Savannah said. "She'll probably think you can't bear to drag yourself out of bed."

Dexter's eyebrows lifted. "*He* will know better. But if the people I was to meet with this morning want to believe otherwise, that's all to the good, don't you think?"

Savannah sighed and went to get her sunglasses and wallet.

Dexter used a key to summon the service elevator, and they left the hotel through a basement entrance next to the laundry. The moist air and the strong scent of de-

tergent made Savannah sneeze, and she hadn't stopped
yet when Dexter unlocked the door of a boxy, dark blue
four-wheel-drive vehicle and helped her into the passenger seat.

"No limo?" she managed to say between sneezes.
"You amaze me."

"Of course not. The limousine comes and goes now
and then, just in case anybody's interested in keeping
tabs on me. But I seldom use it."

"Wait a minute. What good is having a limo parked
in front of the hotel if nobody ever gets in or out of it?
Wouldn't people realize it's a decoy?"

"Oh, there's a private garage in the basement, so all
anyone expects to see is the car."

Savannah remembered the superdark windows and
nodded.

"In the meantime, I'm free to do as I like. Nobody's
going to give me a second look when I'm driving something like this—which is exactly the way I like it."

Mr. Caine prefers his privacy, the bell captain had told
her last night—it *was* just last night, wasn't it? It seemed
a million years ago since he'd taken her up to the suite.
He'd obviously known what he was talking about.
Savannah wouldn't have been surprised to see not only
the limo and chauffeur but an entourage—a couple of
bodyguards, and maybe the secretary, as well.

But now that she was beginning to get a better view
of the man, she realized how appropriate his choice of
transportation was. This was not even the most expensive or luxurious of four-wheel-drive vehicles—just
nice and dependable and unobtrusive.

Nothing at all like the man behind the wheel, who
wasn't nice, wasn't particularly dependable—unless one
counted the fact that he was almost guaranteed to do
the unexpected!—and was certainly not unobtrusive.

Savannah shot a cautious look at him from the corner
of her eye. She could appreciate that on the street, driving

this unlikely vehicle, he might not draw attention—but how did he ever avoid it in a more confined setting? Overlooking him was impossible; he seemed to fill whatever space was available, and he could effortlessly impose his will no matter who else was in the room.

Maybe that was the reason he never seemed to appear in public. If so, being seen with him on a couple of occasions ought to convince even hardened skeptics that there was something serious going on—and then Savannah could go back home, sell her article to Brian....

The magazine might have to run it under a made-up name, though. Savannah could just about imagine the explosion in Las Vegas when Dexter Caine found out about that article, even if it had nothing to do with his little scheme. And of course he would find out.

"Why are you frowning?" he asked. "Are you worried about the paper?"

Before she stopped to think, Savannah asked, "What paper?"

"The newspaper you work for. Are you still with the *Tribune*?"

"Is there any reason you need to know?"

"I thought it might be a good idea if I had some basic information about you."

"Oh, I doubt you're going to send out a press release, so I can't see why you'd need details. And if anybody catches you up short, you can always tell them you've been too fascinated with my body to worry about my mind."

He stopped for a traffic signal and turned to look at her, one eyebrow raised. It was a long red light, and he had plenty of time to look.

Savannah almost asked him to turn the air-conditioning on; she was getting rather warm. Then she realized cool air was already streaming from the vents, and her discomfort had nothing to do with the temperature. Darn it, it wasn't fair that he could have such an incredible impact on her! Of course, she'd been stupid enough to ask for it. "The light's green now," she pointed out.

"Thank you. If your intention was to fascinate me with your body, you certainly started out well last night. Can I expect another installment of the plan soon?"

Savannah wished she'd simply answered the original question; it would have been a lot less painful than changing the subject had turned out to be.

She said firmly, "As long as we're discussing last night, Robinson tells me there's more than one bedroom in the suite. If you've decided you want the one I was using last night, I'll happily move. But I don't plan to share."

He had the grace to look ever so slightly ashamed of himself. "I should have told you that."

"You certainly should have."

"I've found over the years that it's much better to be up-front with information that is bound to come out anyway. Of course, last night it did appear that you didn't want to be alone."

Savannah wasn't going to give him a chance to enlarge on that; it was dead certain she wouldn't come out the winner in that round.

But Dexter wasn't so easily stopped. "In fact I thought for a while last night that you—"

"I'm a free-lancer," she said hastily.

"What?"

"I don't work for one newspaper anymore. I sell to several, and magazines, too."

He smiled lazily, obviously amused by the sudden switch. "Got fired, hmm?"

"I certainly didn't!"

He gave her a disbelieving look. Savannah was annoyed, until she remembered that this line of conversation was a whole lot better than his choice had been.

"I was an investigative reporter in my last regular job," she said. "While I was slogging through an illegal chemical-waste dump one day with rain cascading down the back of my neck, I found myself thinking that there must be an easier way to make a living."

"And is there?"

She raised her chin haughtily. "Of course. I'm doing very well." She thought about her unpaid rent and made a mental note to phone her landlord sometime this weekend. Fortunately, she didn't live in a complex but in a brownstone with just four apartments, and she'd done the owner more than the usual number of favors lately. Jack would probably give her a couple of weeks to catch up.

"In that case I won't worry about paying you," Dexter murmured. "Who were you working for when you chased me down?"

Did he seriously think she'd tell him? "I hadn't sold the idea yet."

She braced herself for another ironic comment, but Dexter was too busy backing into a parking space even to give her a doubting look. He came around to help her out and guided her across the sidewalk to a store.

Savannah took one look at the storefront and stopped dead in her tracks. There wasn't even a name on the door, and in the one window a single dress was displayed. It was a sleek purple satin number, simply cut, very plain, and—Savannah was willing to bet—worth more than her last three months' income. "This is not exactly a discount store."

"Observant, aren't you?"

"I can't afford to shop here."

"Really? I thought you said the free-lance business was doing just fine."

Savannah glared at him. "Obviously not by your standards."

Dexter grinned. "Didn't I tell you this job had certain special benefits?"

"Does that mean you're buying?"

"Don't you think it's obvious that any woman I'd be interested in wouldn't buy her clothes at a discount store? If you turned up togged out in that sort of thing—"

"I suppose you're right," Savannah said airily. "Though it would certainly add emphasis to the claim that you're head over heels in love. Where do you buy your clothes?"

"Are you still playing reporter? Give it up, Savannah."

"You can't refuse to speak to me altogether, you know—silence wouldn't be very convincing to an audience. And the weather is going to be an awfully boring subject after an hour or two. So what are we going to discuss if you won't talk about yourself?"

"We could talk about you. I'd like to hear all about the chemical-waste dump."

"I'll bet. I'm not saying another word about me till I get something about you in return."

"I'm perfectly willing to talk to you. I've already confided my dislike of ostentatious limousines."

"Oh. How thrilling."

Dexter laughed. "That's all you get unless you agree to put every conversation off the record."

Savannah shrugged. "Do I have a choice?"

"That's not good enough. I want an ironclad vow. In fact, I'd prefer a notarized statement." He pulled open the door, and a slender woman in her middle sixties came hurrying toward them.

"Good morning," she said. "What may I help you find?" She inserted a small card in the window. The movement was so smooth that Savannah caught only a glimpse of the card. CLOSED, it said.

Savannah glanced up at Dexter. "Come here often, do you?" she murmured.

That was the last peaceful moment she had for a couple of hours. She was pinned and fitted and paraded around until she couldn't remember any garment she'd tried on. The proprietor and her assistants made Savannah show off every new ensemble to Dexter, though she never saw so much as a flicker of reaction from him. In fact, she'd never seen a man look so bored; he had settled into an upholstered chair with his elbow propped on the arm, his chin in his hand.

It would be no wonder if he was tired, she thought. After all, he'd been up half the night, and it had still been early this morning when Robinson bounded in.... That reminded her of some additional needs.

"Do you have pajamas?" she asked. "And I don't mean negligees, either—just plain ordinary tailored pajamas and a terry robe."

The proprietor smiled. "Certainly, miss." She held out yet another dress. "Let's see if he likes this one, shall we?"

Savannah noticed that the woman had never once used Dexter's name. Did she treat all her customers with this private and personal attention, or was she going to great lengths to protect Dexter Caine's identity?

"I think I've already tried on plenty. I don't need all that much, you know. Besides, he doesn't seem to like anything he's seen so far, so why bother to show him any more?"

The proprietor laughed, and somehow the dress went over Savannah's head and was tugged efficiently into place, and she made another trip to the display room to show Dexter.

"He looks like he's half-asleep," she protested when she was back in the dressing room and they were selecting yet another outfit.

What Savannah didn't say—what she didn't want to admit even to herself—was that his sleepy look made her feel half-naked no matter what she was wearing.

Finally the proprietor said, "I think that takes care of it, Miss Seabrooke."

Savannah, who was standing in the middle of the dressing room wearing only bra and panty hose, sighed in relief. "You've certainly given me plenty to choose from."

It was tempting to order the lot, as long as Dexter was getting the bill. But taking clothes from the man would be accepting a different sort of payoff, so Savannah settled for the minimum. "I think perhaps I'll take the fuchsia dress and the shoes to match, and that pair of cream silk slacks and the matching sweater. That should do it, along with the pajamas and robe... oh, and a couple of sets of underwear. Sort of basic stuff—nothing too fancy—so it can go under anything."

The proprietor nodded. "Certainly," she said. "I'll have the things delivered, shall I? Unless you'd like to wear the slacks outfit?"

Savannah put down the pair of jeans she'd just picked up. "Good idea," she said. "You don't know how tired I am of wearing these. After two days without a change of clothes—" Too late, she realized it wasn't a particularly smart statement. "The airlines are so careless, you know," she added, and hoped that nobody here knew about Dexter's private plane.

I'm not cut out for this kind of intrigue, she thought, and longed for the day when she could go back to picking holes in other people's stories instead of guarding her own tongue all the time. How long might that be? Two days? Three?

Surely, she thought, it couldn't be much longer than that.

Savannah was quiet on the way back to the hotel, conscious that this might be one of the few chances she'd get to see anything of Las Vegas. Even at midday, the casinos along the Strip glittered with light and their neon signs beckoned all comers. "I didn't expect it to be so busy," she said.

"It isn't, compared to later in the evening."

"I suppose not," she said slowly, "but I guess I thought it would be—I don't know—more *normal* at this time of day."

"People on vacation don't care what time of day it is. And Las Vegas never stops, you know. There are deals going down all the time."

"Is that what you were doing last night? Putting together some sort of big deal? Or were you just playing craps or the slot machines or something?"

Dexter smiled. "Is there a difference?"

"You're not going to talk to me, are you?"

"I'm still holding out for a notarized statement that you won't use anything I say." He walked her to the door of the suite and unlocked it. "See you tonight. I think perhaps we'll have dinner downstairs, too. Can you be ready by seven?"

"That's only eight hours," Savannah said. "But I'll try to whip myself into decent shape by then."

Robinson was nowhere in sight, and the suite was quiet except for the hum of the air-conditioning and a vague noise that might have been traffic on the street far below. The day stretched emptily in front of her. Dexter wouldn't be back till seven....

Now that was a downright silly reaction, she thought. She had her computer, and it was a luxury to have a whole day to work without interruption. It was dead sure she wasn't going to be getting phone calls!

She headed for her bedroom to unpack the computer. It took her a moment to realize that in one corner of the room was a new addition—a big, deep armchair upholstered in pewter-colored velvet. Beside it was a tall lamp with a powerful bulb.

She tried out the chair and discovered gleefully that it was as comfortable as it looked. She went looking for

Robinson, and found him in the kitchen, testing an iron with his fingertip. On the board in front of him lay—

She blinked in astonishment. "What are you doing?"

"I'm pressing your newspaper, miss."

"I can see that. Why? Was it wrinkled?"

"Oh, no. The heat sets the ink so it won't rub off on your fingers."

"Really? Aren't you a dear? It's awfully nice of you to get my chair and lamp so quickly. I'd hug you for it, but I'm afraid I'd offend your dignity."

To her fascination, his face flushed a little and he stepped back as if afraid she'd do so anyway. "I only did as you wished, miss."

"I see. You're some sort of genie who can do anything."

He unbent enough to smile. "Not quite, though Mr. Caine does say sometimes...." He stopped discreetly. "But I shouldn't talk about him."

Utterly fascinated, Savannah perched on the edge of the counter and folded her arms. "You're not talking about him," she pointed out. "You're telling me about you. What does he say?"

"He's been kind enough to comment that occasionally I can pull off something he thought impossible."

"Like....?"

"Very dull things, I'm afraid. Like convincing an Irish electrician to install American-style wiring in the manor house in County Cork so Mr. Caine could use the electronics equipment he prefers."

"He's got a manor house in Ireland?"

"Yes, miss. Only a small one, I might add."

"You mean it doesn't have its own butler?"

He obviously didn't miss the faint irony in her tone. "Mr. Caine has chosen to have only one."

"That must keep you busy."

"I'm flattered that he's put his faith in me. Each house has its own staff, of course, which keeps things operating when I'm not present."

"Of course," Savannah murmured.

"The hotel suites are a little different, since there's so much support staff readily available."

"How sensible."

"But I consider my duties to be very simple. I carry out Mr. Caine's wishes. And those of his guests, of course."

It certainly *sounded* simple, but Savannah suspected it hardly ever was. "Well, I'm overwhelmed. If I start overdoing the wishes, let me know, all right?"

Robinson allowed himself a very slight smile. "I think that's doubtful, miss." He refolded the newspaper and presented it to her with a tiny bow. "While you have a moment, may I ask if there is anything particular you'd like for your lunch?"

Savannah ran a finger deliberately across the banner headline and checked her fingertip. Sure enough, there wasn't a trace of ink. "Oh, let's see...something exotic, so I can watch you wave the magic wand and get it."

"I'm afraid if it's too exotic I'll merely call down to the restaurant."

"Oh. I'm heartbroken to hear that, you know. Tell you what—just put some cheese between two slices of bread and iron it."

His composure cracked a bit. "What?"

"Don't you know the lazy way to make a grilled cheese sandwich, Robinson? As good as you are with an iron, I'm amazed you hadn't discovered that. All the girls in my college dorm knew it."

"Yes, miss," he said faintly.

Savannah gave him a friendly grin and went back to her bedroom to unpack her computer. It ought to be interesting to see what he actually produced when lunchtime came, she thought.

A little later, Robinson tapped on her door, and when she answered, he came in carrying a stack of dress boxes.

Savannah looked up from the computer screen, where she was doing a final revision of an article on hospice care. Then she took off her reading glasses and looked again. "What's all that?"

"The delivery from the boutique, miss."

"But I didn't buy all that."

"Apparently Mr. Caine did. He seems to have signed the sales order, at least." He turned on his heel and went back to the living room, returning a moment later with yet another stack of boxes.

Savannah was speechless. She would have sworn Dexter hadn't indicated a shred of interest in anything she'd modeled. Were these his choices, or the proprietor's? She started opening boxes in amazement.

The fuchsia dinner dress she'd chosen was there, and the plain and simple underwear she'd requested, and the pajamas and robe. But there were also a dozen more dresses and a full wardrobe of skirts and slacks and sweaters and blouses and lingerie and shoes....

Unpacking was like a little girl's dress-up dreams come true, till suddenly Savannah sat down in the midst of the heaps of lovely fabrics and put both hands to her temples.

Just how many clothes did Dexter Caine expect her to need anyway? And—more importantly—just how long did he intend this masquerade to go on?

CHAPTER FOUR

SAVANNAH was just smoothing her hair into an elegant French twist when Robinson knocked on her bedroom door. "Mr. Caine is waiting, miss."

She glanced at the clock. "Mr. Caine is early," she pointed out. "Tell him I'll be just a minute. Were you able to find the ribbon I wanted?"

"No, miss. I'm sorry."

He sounded it, too, as if admitting failure was almost more than he could bear.

Savannah plunged the last hairpin into place and inspected herself in the mirror. The fuchsia dress fit like a dream, and the matching pumps made her feel six inches taller and very elegant. The tiny pearl earrings she'd been wearing since Chicago were far too dainty to balance the elegance of the dress, but that couldn't be helped; they were the only jewelry she had. It was too bad she didn't have her heavy gold necklace. It wasn't truly gold, of course, only gold-colored, but from a distance nobody could tell, and it would have showed off perfectly against the heart-shaped neckline.

But of course she wasn't in the habit of carrying her jewelry around with her. When she'd realized half an hour ago just how bare the neckline looked, she'd called Robinson in a panic, hoping he could get a wide strip of fuchsia velvet ribbon to tie around her throat. He'd certainly managed to find the makeup she needed on short notice, but she'd thought of that a couple of hours earlier. She probably shouldn't have specified fuchsia ribbon, she realized. Black might have worked, as well, and would have been a great deal easier to locate. But it was too late now.

Savannah picked up the tiny evening bag that matched the dress and touched her hair one last time. Her fingers were trembling just a little, and there was a flutter of nervousness at the pit of her stomach.

Think of it as a blind date, she told herself, and you'll be just fine. The image of Dexter as an unknown man she didn't especially want to be with, but whom she absolutely had to impress, helped a little to ease her jitters.

Dexter was in the living room, leaning over a sofa table reading the newspaper she'd left there. The whisper of her silk skirt in the quiet room made him look up, and Savannah almost gasped as she got her first good look at him in evening clothes. Last night hadn't counted, for he hadn't been wearing his jacket.

She'd never even seen a photograph of him in a tuxedo, she realized, and wondered why the paparazzi had never managed to catch him looking like this. The severe black and white accented his dark hair and richly tanned skin and made his eyes appear even larger. He looked absolutely wonderful.

And what, she wondered, did he think of her?

This morning in the boutique, even though he'd appeared to be half-asleep, she'd felt as if she was on display. It had been an uncomfortable feeling—an odd mix of excitement and trepidation. But that was nothing to the sensation that swept over her now. She hadn't realized till this moment just how bare the low neckline really was, or how the slim skirt molded itself against her hips. Every cell felt aflame under his inspection.

This is ridiculous, Savannah told herself. There was nothing remotely sensual about the way he was looking her over, and only an overactive imagination would even dream there was anything going on but calm appraisal. But those dark eyes sweeping from her blond hair to the toes of her elegant shoes left her feeling anything but calm.

Of course he was taking a good look. It wasn't unreasonable for him to inspect her and make sure she wasn't going to embarrass him in what was shaping up to be the kookiest scheme of the decade. Better to find out right now that her hair was falling down or she had a scrap of tissue paper stuck to the bottom of her shoe than to discover it downstairs amid a crowd of interested onlookers. She couldn't blame Dexter for looking.

What was insane was the way she was reacting. It was only her fancy that said his gaze seemed to linger at the base of her throat, where she could feel her pulse flickering.... Breathless panic began to throb along each nerve. What did he think? What would he say?

Dexter looked her over slowly once more, then pushed the paper aside and straightened up. "You'll do," he said calmly. "I thought you would."

I was right, Savannah thought. That whole survey had been completely meaningless. And she was glad; things could have become very uncomfortable if Dexter had found her attractive. Under the circumstances ... well, she didn't even want to think about that.

Still, there was an odd flat sensation in the pit of her stomach. Surely it wasn't disappointment? How utterly foolish she was being; she simply had to get control of her overactive imagination.

"Good," she said acidly. "I'd so hate to have you send me back to Chicago tonight in disfavor."

Dexter smiled, and his eyes took on a lighter glow like the gleam of amber. "Frankly, I wouldn't have been a bit surprised if you'd tried to accomplish precisely that."

"And miss this wonderful opportunity?" Her voice was dry. "Since I doubt it would have done me any good—"

"You're quite right. It wouldn't."

"I've decided to make the best of this lucky break, Mr. Caine."

His eyebrows rose slightly at the undeniable irony in her voice. "Lucky break? What an interesting way of looking at it. Don't you think, by the way, that you'd better start using my name?"

"Actually, I thought I'd skip that stage altogether." Savannah fluttered a hand at him as if inviting him to kiss her fingers. "Other titles seem to fit you so much better—darling."

"Watch that you don't overdo it, Savannah." He moved the newspaper aside and picked up a black velvet box, which had been half-hidden underneath. "This is why Robinson didn't get your ribbon."

"And I thought he was so stiff because he hates admitting failure."

He snapped open the lid and turned the box toward her. Indirect light from the wall sconces bounced and shattered off a twisted rope of fiery stones, and Savannah gasped.

"Don't get any ideas," Dexter said coolly. "This is borrowed from the shop in the lobby, and it goes back tomorrow."

She didn't even want to touch the necklace. "I hope you borrowed a bodyguard to go with it."

"Of course not. If the necklace disappears, I won't have any trouble proving grand theft, and all my troubles will be over." He lifted the diamond necklace from the pale blue satin that lined the box.

The gold was chilly against Savannah's skin, and the facets of the diamonds on the very edges of the necklace felt almost sharp as he slipped it around her throat and fastened the safety clasp. The cool weight and the knowledge of the sheer value of the necklace sent shivers down her spine. Or else... but surely she wasn't reacting to the brush of his fingers, warm and smooth against her nape!

"Of course, you'd still have Cassie King to worry about," she said.

"True." He removed one of her pearl earrings and slid one single enormous diamond into its place. Savannah got a quick look at it; the stone was as big as her smallest fingernail.

"Wouldn't it be easier just to talk to her? Tell her to cut out the nonsense, I mean, instead of pulling off this stunt."

He picked up the second earring. "Don't you think I've tried? Cassie can be remarkably obtuse."

"Unless Cassie's just an excuse, and your real goal is to get even with the press by making fools of them," Savannah murmured.

"You can't imagine I'd admit that to you. In any case, if you're thinking of calling Cassie up to tell her all about us, don't bother. She started a new concert tour this week."

"Really? Is that why you're in such a hurry to get this scheme underway—because her back is turned for the moment?"

"Who says I'm in a hurry?"

"Come on, Dexter." She tightened the diamond earrings till they pinched her earlobes. That way, if the darned things fell off she'd know immediately. "You were even willing to accept a substitute rather than wait for your first choice to be available."

"And see how wonderfully it's working out? Not every woman would be so able to entertain herself when I'm busy—but your mind never stops racing, does it?"

She looked up at him warily. If he had any idea what kinds of wild thoughts were running through her head....

"Of course," Dexter murmured, "sometimes your mind goes around in unfathomable circles. Just in case you're thinking of causing a little sabotage this evening, Savannah, I wouldn't advise it."

She breathed a little more easily. "Oh, warnings aren't necessary. You expressed yourself very clearly this morning about the consequences if I didn't behave."

"That's good."

"Besides, I wouldn't dream of leaving you prematurely." She gave him a sunny smile. "Don't forget I'm holding out for the authorized biography."

He offered his arm. "And I'm waiting for the notarized statement."

"Then we understand each other very well," Savannah murmured. It was silly to hesitate before taking his arm, she told herself. Simply touching the man wasn't going to electrocute her! She tucked a hand into his elbow and fluttered her eyelashes at him. "Don't we, darling?"

"We do, indeed." They strolled across the small lobby from the penthouse door to the elevator. Its engraved brass doors were highly polished, though the mirror effect was dim and distorted. Still, the diamond necklace reflected brightly.

I suppose you get used to this sort of thing, Savannah thought, and wondered once more how long she was apt to be playing the part. "The regular elevator?" she said as the car slid to a smooth and silent stop and the doors opened invitingly. "Oh, of course—it *is* a special occasion."

"We're celebrating...what, do you think?" Dexter pushed the button for the main lobby level and turned to Savannah, head tipped inquiringly.

Savannah considered. "The one-month anniversary of our meeting?"

"That seems reasonable. Much longer than that, and there would be questions about why no one had seen you before."

"Is that how you keep your women under wraps?" Savannah asked innocently. "By limiting all relationships to thirty days?"

Dexter's eyes narrowed. "Not at all," he murmured. "I do it by *not* behaving like this."

His arm slid around her, hard and unyielding as steel. Obviously he worked out with weights, Savannah noted in the last millisecond of sanity before his mouth claimed hers.

Last night she'd awakened while he was kissing her, aware only that she'd never known such an expert caress, and she'd reacted like butter melting into a pancake. If she'd thought about it—which she hadn't—she'd have assumed that it had taken a bit of time to build that level of excitement, till the sensation broke through her subconscious mind and brought her to total awareness.

Now she discovered that all it took was the first kiss, for the instant his lips met hers, her knees dissolved.

Dexter knew it, too. He had to know it, for only the grip of his strong arms held her upright.

His kiss was neither brutal nor insensitive, but it was merciless. He robbed Savannah of breath, of the power of movement—and of free will. She could no more have torn herself from his arms than she could have flown down from the penthouse balcony.

Her heart seemed to jolt, but it took her a moment to realize the sensation wasn't the panic she felt but the elevator stopping. She murmured something against his lips—a protest, she hoped—but he didn't let her go. Instead, he held her just far enough away so he could pull the silk handkerchief from the breast pocket of his tuxedo, and he used the edge of it to feather the corners of her mouth.

She looked up at him in confusion, wondering what he was doing—and how it was possible that the touch of silk wrapped around his finger was almost as intimate a caress as the kiss itself had been.

"I smeared your lipstick," he whispered. "Now I'm fixing it so you don't have to—because I don't want to let you go for a moment."

She blinked up at him in wonder. Then something moved outside the elevator, and she realized Dexter was playing to an audience—a fascinated one, to judge by the number of slightly open mouths.

He followed her gaze. "Sorry, darling." His voice was low and throaty, but she suspected it carried just as far as he intended it to. "I know how much you hate public scenes. I was . . . overwhelmed."

How on earth was she supposed to answer that? And why—considering the circumstances—was she wasting time wondering how he acted when he was *really* overwhelmed, not just acting the part? "We're holding up the elevator," she managed.

"It's my elevator. I'll hold it up just as long as I want to."

He might have sounded like a petulant child, Savannah thought, except that his voice throbbed with desire. At least, if she hadn't known better, she'd have thought that was what it was—and no doubt the people waiting outside were convinced. A couple of the women sighed romantically. Savannah closed her eyes in frustration.

But he let her go, steadying her with one hand on her elbow while with the other he raised the handkerchief to his own mouth to remove the traces of her lipstick.

Savannah couldn't bring herself to congratulate him on a master performance, so they crossed the lobby in almost complete silence, past the great glass doors that led into the casino, to the main dining room. Dexter fiddled with his handkerchief the whole way, paying no attention to the interest of onlookers, and was just tucking the silk square back into his breast pocket when the maître d' stepped into the arched doorway of the hotel's elegant main restaurant to greet them. Savannah thought the man's eyes were about to pop.

"Your usual table, Mr. Caine?"

Dexter wasn't even looking at the man; he was still studying Savannah with what looked like mad passion in his eyes. "No," he said thoughtfully. "Something with a better view tonight. The lady likes to watch people."

"Thanks for filling me in on my little quirks," Savannah muttered. She followed the maître d'.

Dexter trailed a couple of steps behind. Savannah could actually feel the way his gaze lingered over her, for the sensation was almost as warm as a physical touch.

The maître d' paused by a small table nearly at dead center of the room and pulled out a chair. Suddenly Dexter was beside her again, waving the man away and holding her chair himself.

As if he can't stand to have another man perform such a personal service for me, Savannah thought.

At least it must have looked that way to every woman in the restaurant. Suddenly it seemed to her that there must be hundreds, and every one of them was staring in her direction.

Dexter's hands slid from the tall back of her chair up over her shoulders with a feather-light touch. He hesitated for an instant, as if he was considering bending over to kiss the nape of her neck, and then stepped away to take his own chair next to hers.

Savannah picked up her napkin. For two cents, she thought, she'd drape it over her head, slink out, and not stop walking till she got back to Chicago. But she didn't think Dexter would hesitate to carry out his threats. Backing down wasn't his style, and now she had personal evidence that he didn't easily lose his nerve—he hadn't even paused for consideration before he'd kissed her with the intimacy of a longtime lover in front of a whole lobby full of people.

How had he dared anyway? What had made him so sure that she wouldn't scream and kick him and run? He'd given her hardly an instant's warning, and in those circumstances even the best actress might not pull off the performance of her life. Dexter Caine must be even more of a gambler than Savannah had thought.

She glanced around and noticed that the tables were carefully placed, just a little too far apart for a conversation held in normal tones to be overheard. That was a blessing. She smiled brilliantly at Dexter and said, "What were you trying to prove back there in the elevator?"

"I told you. That was a demonstration of how not to avoid attention."

"Well, I don't want another like it. Ever!"

"You didn't enjoy it? Well, I suppose that's your right. It was very effective, however. Wouldn't you agree?"

Savannah ignored him. "If you absolutely must do that again—"

"You mean kiss you?" Dexter said helpfully. "You can say the word openly, Savannah. I promise I won't be shocked."

"You will give me fair warning ahead of time, and you will be gentle. I'm bruised from that manhandling."

He leaned forward till his eyes—which looked suddenly darker, more intense and sincere—were mere inches from hers. His fingers cupped her chin and tipped her face up for a better look, and his gaze came to rest on her lips.

Savannah tried to draw back. His fingers tightened ever so slightly on her chin and drew her closer yet. He looked as if he intended to kiss her all over again. So much for her demand for fair warning, Savannah thought. Unless he actually thought that gazing soulfully into her eyes was notice enough!

Her lips itched under his intense gaze, and she willed herself not to lick them.

"I don't see any bruises," Dexter murmured. He let her go, his fingers slipping very slowly down her throat as if he was reluctant to lose contact.

"Not there," she said. Her voice didn't seem to work right, either. "As I was going to tell you, my ribs feel cracked."

"Oh. Well, I can hardly check that out here, can I?" He picked up her hand instead and held it between his. For a moment, the hypnotic rhythm of his fingertips stroking the back of her hand, combined with the dark steadiness of his gaze, made Savannah feel a little dizzy. Dexter turned his head. The soft pattern of stroking did not vary. "Ah, Raoul. You're back to work already?"

A waiter stood beside the table. Savannah was startled; she hadn't caught even a flicker of movement, and yet there he was, standing silently with his hands clasped behind his back, as if he was prepared to wait forever.

"Yes, sir," he said slowly. "But I was gone six weeks, you know."

"Has it been that long? Not that I didn't miss you. How's the little girl?"

"The therapist says she'll be perfectly fine. Sir—"

"That's good." Dexter turned to Savannah. "Raoul's daughter was hit by a car. Fortunately, there's a really good rehabilitation center here, and they had a bed open, so she's getting the best of care."

The waiter stood a little taller. "Sir, I wanted to say—"

Dexter murmured, "I think the lady's hungry, Raoul. What do you recommend tonight?"

Raoul gave a tiny sigh. "As you like, sir. The chef has a very nice duckling this evening," he murmured. "Also a prize bit of venison. Of course, if the lady prefers seafood or poultry for her main course...."

Savannah knew only two things; she was seriously out of her depth, and there wasn't a menu to be seen. She shot a pleading look at Dexter and said, "You choose." The words came out too harsh, too blunt, and she added breathlessly, "You always do such a wonderful job of pleasing me, darling."

Dexter smiled—the kind of self-assured smile that unabashedly agreed with her opinion—and said, "I do my best, my dear...in everything."

Savannah knew she shouldn't have been surprised at that particular double meaning—it was so obvious that he must have thought she'd given him the opening on purpose. Still, she couldn't help feeling that the room had suddenly gotten just a little too warm for comfort.

He turned back to the waiter. "We'll have the duckling, with the nest of quail's eggs and shrimp to start. And probably the Cointreau strawberries later."

The waiter's eyes rested speculatively on Savannah. "Would you like champagne with the strawberries, sir?"

"Of course. Nothing else is quite suitable for a celebration."

"And the other wines?"

Dexter waved a hand as if the subject bored him. "Tell the wine steward I'd rather not be bothered with a list. He knows the kind of thing I like."

"Then I shall consult him and see to it."

"You do that. You're a good man, Raoul." He began stroking Savannah's hand again; she withdrew it and reached for her water goblet. Dexter sat back in his chair, smiling slightly.

"What was that all about?" Savannah asked.

"What do you mean?"

"Raoul and his little girl. Obviously he was trying to tell you something."

"Was he? I haven't the vaguest idea what it might have been. I'll have to ask him someday."

It was the first time Savannah had seen him look the slightest bit uncomfortable. It might be interesting, she thought, to find out just how the rehab center had happened to have a bed open at the moment it was needed. It was dead sure, however, that Dexter wasn't going to tell her, so she changed the subject. "You're not a wine connoisseur?"

"I know quite a little about wines, but I've found it's a mistake to order specific ones, at least in restaurants that I patronize a great deal."

Savannah frowned. "Why? I should think—"

"The wine steward always knows the best of what his cellar holds, but that choice is not always obvious from his list. Sometimes the best aren't on the list at all."

"Why wouldn't they be?"

"Because they're too newly acquired, or he could get only a very limited supply, or he's holding the last few bottles of a prized vintage for very special customers who appreciate quality. Who knows why? At any rate, I've found it much wiser to throw myself on his mercy—after first making sure, of course, that he realizes I am one of those very special customers." The wine steward appeared, napkin-wrapped bottle in hand, and poured a trickle of white wine into Dexter's glass. Dexter picked it up, swirled the liquid, inhaled, tasted, and nodded. "Very nice."

"It's a personal favorite of mine, sir." The steward filled Savannah's glass, topped off Dexter's, set the bottle into a silver stand at Dexter's elbow, and vanished.

"You see?" Dexter said. "No fuss, and only a moment's interruption instead of a long lecture about aroma and bouquet."

"I thought they were the same thing."

"Don't tell the wine steward that, or he'll never leave." He raised his glass to Savannah. "Shall we drink to a wonderful month just past?"

I can wholeheartedly agree with that, Savannah thought. At least nine-tenths of the previous month had been not bad at all—right up to the past couple of days, in fact. "And let's drink to another one just like it to come," she mused, and added, under her breath, "Soon, I hope."

Dexter laughed. "I thought you'd resigned yourself to sticking around. The biography, you know."

"Oh, *resigned* is hardly the right word. It's just that I need to make some plans. How long do you expect I'll have to gather my material?"

He shrugged. "Haven't the foggiest."

"Oh, come on. You must have some idea how long this is going to take. You bought more clothes than I've ever owned in my life."

"How do you know they're not simply borrowed, too?"

"Because Robinson told me you signed a sales ticket. Unless you're planning to return what I don't use? Now that's an ingenious idea—buy more than you expect to need, so there's plenty of choice, and just send the rest back."

"Repeated trips are such a waste of time," he agreed. "Still, I expect you'll need most everything."

Savannah gulped a little. "Everything?"

"Surely you don't think any woman I was interested in would appear more than once in any dress, do you?" His voice was bland.

If he really meant that—which she wasn't at all sure was the case—it should have been some comfort. Still, as Savannah tried to count up the number of outfits now hanging behind that long row of closet doors in her bedroom, she realized that even by Dexter Caine's rules he'd bought her enough clothes for three weeks.

"What's the matter, Savannah?" he asked solicitously. "Aren't you as interested in the biography as you thought you were?"

She gave him a brilliant smile. "Actually, I'm eager to get into my research."

"Are you, now?" His voice reminded her of the touch of his silk handkerchief against her lips. It was just as soft and smooth—though there was a hint of danger underneath. "Perhaps I should be asking what sort of research you have in mind."

"Not the kind you're thinking of," Savannah said tartly, and was annoyed with herself when Dexter laughed. When would she learn to stop taking the bait?

She seized the opportunity to study the dining room. The arched ceiling stretched twenty feet above her head, supported by pink marble columns that divided the enormous space into several more intimate areas, separated in places by a couple of shallow steps or planters full of lush greenery. The room, like the few other bits of the hotel she'd managed to see, was huge and elegant and stunning—but in Las Vegas, the city of spectacle, it was nothing much at all.

Every year brought at least one more new and glamorous resort to the Strip. The stakes got higher every year, the architecture more exotic, the themes more outlandish, in an effort to draw patrons not only with gambling but also with scenery.

Beside that competition, Savannah wondered, how could an ordinary hotel—no matter how elegant— survive? And why had Dexter Caine wanted it?

"How did you end up with this hotel?" she asked.

"Is this a research question, Savannah?"

"There's some speculation that you won it playing roulette."

The waiter set a plain china plate in front of her. On it were three circles of twisted greenery. One held a tiny hard-boiled egg, which had been cut into quarters, one contained several boiled shrimp, which were glossy with marinade, and one was filled with something that could only be caviar.

I'm not cut out for this kind of living, Savannah thought. She'd never tasted caviar, and she wasn't eager to try it now.

Dexter spread caviar on a toast point. "Really? I hadn't heard that one."

The statement was neither confirmation nor denial, Savannah realized. She persisted, mostly because she had nothing better to do. "What are you going to do with it? It's a strange possession for you."

"Oh, if you think this is strange, you should see some of my other investments."

"I'd love to. Is that an invitation to tour them all?"

"Don't be silly, Savannah. Do go on. I'm finding your logic fascinating."

She stabbed a shrimp. "There's no question it's prime real estate," she mused. "Even though the hotel is close to forty years old, it's...."

"Yes?"

"Sitting on a gold mine," she finished triumphantly. "The *land*. There's plenty of it, and it's one of the best locations in the city. You're going to tear the hotel down and build a resort, aren't you?"

"Lower your voice, dear," he said gently. "I wouldn't want all the waiters to think they'll be out of jobs by morning. It would be such a tacky way to spread the news."

"Then I'm right?" She abandoned her appetizer and leaned forward, eyes wide with anticipation. "What are you going to build instead, Dexter?"

"I wouldn't want to ruin your fun by telling you. I'm sure you'd rather figure it out for yourself."

"It's going to have to be something really eye-catching, really exotic, to stand out in this environment. A Greek temple, maybe? Or a re-creation of the Hanging Gardens of Babylon? King Kong's island? Whatever it is, it'll have to be out of this world."

"How'd you guess?"

Savannah stopped dead. What did I miss? she thought.

Dexter's gaze was level, clear, perfectly straightforward.

"Out of this world," she repeated slowly. "You mean—like a space station or something?"

"Oh, no. We considered it, but the problem of simulating zero gravity was too much for the engineers to overcome."

"Then what? The moon?"

"Mars, actually. Don't you think it's exciting? The guests can get around via the canals—"

"Mars doesn't really have canals. Not water-filled ones, at least."

Dexter shrugged. "Did I say we were going to use water?"

"And I suppose you're going to call the main lounge the Space Bar? Dammit, Dexter, you're pulling my leg, aren't you?"

"Well, yes," he said soberly. "But it seemed to be what you wanted. Do you always throw yourself into your work like this?"

Savannah's pride was still stinging from having taken him seriously even for an instant. "Why do you want to know?" she grumbled.

"Just making conversation."

"That's not fair. You can ask whatever you want, and I can't."

He smiled. "Oh, you can *ask*. What newspapers and magazines do you work for mostly?"

"Just interested? Or looking for a way to get me fired?"

"I thought free-lancers couldn't be fired."

She let that one pass. The waiter removed her appetizer and replaced it with an elegant serving of roast duckling, the slices arranged in a perfect fan shape on the china plate, with brilliant-hued baby vegetables on the side. The food was beautiful, but she had no appetite.

"You know," she said thoughtfully, "I think Robinson has potential."

Dexter's eyebrows soared. "I beg your pardon?"

"He served me the most magnificent grilled cheese sandwich for lunch." Savannah poked at her food. "I'm sure this is tasty, but now that I think about actually eating a baby duck, I'm considering becoming a vegetarian."

"Watch out," Dexter warned in a low voice. "Cameras off to the left."

She didn't look up. "It took them long enough. Why do they have to appear when we've just started to eat?"

"I suspect it's because that makes the most unflattering pictures."

She speared a tender pea pod and offered it to Dexter. "Shall we give them something better to snap?"

"Why not?" He caught her wrist lightly and nibbled at the vegetable.

Savannah tried to ignore the intimate pressure of his fingers against the pulse point in her wrist. "That reminds me. I don't think I've ever seen a picture of you in a tux in any of the tabloids."

"Read them a lot, do you?"

Better watch out for slips of the tongue, Savannah, she warned herself. "Do you have any ideas on how to avoid them? They're always staring customers in the face in the grocery checkout lane, and you're on the front page pretty regularly."

"You could stop going to the grocery store."

"That's easy for you to say. You have Robinson."

"Eat out, then." He poked through the pile of vegetables on his plate. "Do you like red peppers?"

"Not well enough to eat yours as well as my own." She cautiously tried a bite of the duckling. "You never answered my question about the tuxedo. And why would they want unflattering pictures of you anyway?"

"Because it fits the image they like—dark and gangsterish, difficult and mysterious. Apparently I look a little too sophisticated in a tux."

He could say that again. "Is that why you're always scowling, too? They won't publish happy pictures?"

"Not entirely. I do that on purpose whenever I catch sight of a camera. It's cheap entertainment for me, and it keeps them happy. Tonight's an exception, of course." The way he smiled at her made Savannah's toes curl in shock. He was looking into her eyes as if he found her the most fascinating woman on earth. "If you don't want the duckling, Savannah—"

"Actually, I don't want anything. I'd rather not pick up next week's *Informant* and see myself on the front page, chewing." From the corner of her eye she spotted the photographer moving closer, and she leaned toward Dexter to coo, "Besides, being with you is the only nourishment I crave."

Dexter smothered a chuckle by picking up her hand and burying his mouth in her palm. His breath tickled her lifeline and sent flickers of electricity up her arm. Only an effort of will—and the knowledge that the camera would capture any move she made—allowed Savannah to sit perfectly still.

The photographer eased up to the table. His camera was balanced in one hand, down by his side, though its lens was still aimed squarely at the two of them. Savannah noted also that he stopped just a little more than arm's length from the table.

He was clearly experienced in his line of work, she concluded. It made sense not to shove a camera directly into the subject's face, and it was even smarter—when the subject was as obviously strong and active as Dexter Caine—to keep a discreet distance.

The photographer's voice was so smooth it barely escaped being oily. "I'm sure you'd like your privacy tonight, sir."

Dexter looked at him as if he'd climbed out of a drain somewhere and was still covered with slime. "You're quite correct," he said coolly. "And if you don't go away right now...."

The photographer smiled slyly. "I'll be happy to leave you alone, if perhaps I could have just one small piece of information in exchange for disappearing."

Dexter looked at him for a long moment through half-hooded eyes. "And what's that?"

"The lady's name, sir."

Dexter let Savannah's hand slip from his with what looked like reluctance, and pushed his chair away from the table.

Savannah saw the photographer swallow hard and take a tiny step back. She didn't blame him; she wouldn't have been surprised to see him cut and run entirely.

But Dexter didn't get up. He raised a hand instead, and the maître d' and three waiters, who had converged on the table, paused just out of reach of the photographer.

"I suppose that's not unreasonable," Dexter murmured. "Very well. Her name is...." He turned to look at Savannah.

The softness in his eyes brought a lump to her throat, even though she knew it was only a gimmick for the photographer's sake.

Dexter reached for her hand again and said softly, "Just call her Mrs. Caine."

CHAPTER FIVE

DEXTER'S hand had tightened on Savannah's, but the warning wasn't necessary; she was too frozen to move at all.

And to think, Savannah told herself, that earlier in the evening she'd been so embarrassed she'd considered slinking out of the restaurant with a napkin over her head. What had been the big deal anyway? She couldn't even remember at the moment, though she knew darned well it paled beside this prank. What had inspired the man to claim they were already married anyway?

She heard the camera click and hoped that her shock didn't show in her face. She turned away, staring at the slices of duckling congealing on her plate. It was a good thing she'd already given up on dinner; she positively couldn't eat anything now.

"How did you two meet, Mrs. Caine?" the photographer asked silkily.

"The deal included one question," Dexter reminded him. "And you've had your answer."

At a jerk of Dexter's head, the maître d' stepped up to the photographer and murmured something.

The photographer smiled. "I'll go, since you insist, Mr. Caine," he murmured. "But it's not so easy to get rid of me altogether." He slouched out of the room.

Slowly the restaurant came to life again, and the silence filled once more with the click of plates, the murmur of conversations. Most of the patrons were still looking at Dexter and Savannah, however.

"What...." Savannah's voice stuck in her throat, and she had to cough before she could try again. "What in heaven's name made you tell him we were married, Dexter?''

"I didn't. It's a somewhat technical point, I admit, but I didn't actually say you're my wife. There could be a lot of Mrs. Caines."

"It's more than *somewhat* technical! What other conclusion could he possibly draw?"

"Well, I doubt he'll consider the possibility that you're my mother," Dexter admitted. "Personally, I think it was a brilliant inspiration."

"You could have warned me! What if I'd gone sliding out of my chair in shock? What a picture that would have made for the tabloids!"

Dexter looked interested. "It would, actually. I'd have just scooped you up in my arms and blamed the photographer for your faint—heartlessly intruding on our privacy like that."

"I'm touched," Savannah muttered. "Haven't we had this conversation once already—about warning me before you pull some incredible stunt?"

"Oh, I wasn't worried about your losing your cool, no matter what I said. You're a trouper, you know that, Savannah?"

He sounded quite pleased with her, and with himself, Savannah thought wildly. She considered dumping the contents of her wineglass over his head, just to see whether that would make her point. "Tell me, did you even weigh the consequences of an announcement like that, or did you do this entirely on the spur of the moment?"

"Of course I considered what would happen. Just think of how busy the tabloid people will be, searching for the record of our secret marriage so they can print all the details. They'll start here in Vegas, of course, and when they don't find anything, they'll work their way out across the country. And since there's nothing to find, they'll have to search through every county courthouse in the United States to be sure they haven't missed the license." He sounded as if the prospect pleased him.

Savannah was staring at him in disbelief. "I hate to disillusion you, Dexter, but they're far more likely to just make something up and credit it to a source who doesn't want to be identified. You're apt to read in next week's *Informant* that we were married by a guru while hanging upside down from Mount McKinley."

"Oh?" He looked interested. "Have you done a lot of research on how the tabloids get their so-called news?"

Savannah countered, "Don't you think that much is obvious? Or haven't you ever read them at all?" Before he could pursue the question, she added quickly, "Or else they could just retrace your trail for the past few weeks."

Dexter shook his head. "That won't get them anywhere."

"It also won't keep them busy for long, and if they can establish there's no license anywhere you've been lately—"

"You might be surprised, but tracing me isn't easily done. I've been crisscrossing the country for most of the past month."

"On purpose, no doubt—getting ready for this stunt?"

"Oh, no. It was all legitimate business. But how long does it take to get married anyway? All I had to do was drop out of sight for a couple of hours, and they haven't a clue about when or where I might have done so. No, they'll be busy for weeks chasing a phantom marriage license."

"Not too busy to bother us," Savannah said dryly. "I'd count on that much."

Dexter shrugged. "That is the point after all—to keep their attention firmly focused on us. Without that announcement tonight, our little romance would no doubt get some idle speculation next week, and probably a little more in the issue after that. As it is, I've guaranteed us the front page of the next issue of every tabloid in North America. And since I'm not in the mood to wait forever for results from this stunt...."

"That makes two of us." Savannah pushed her plate away. "Why are you doing this anyway? That's what I'd like to know. I mean, the tabloids have been taking cheap shots at you for years, and you've never blown a gasket before. Why now? Never mind—I know you won't tell me."

The waiter appeared. "There is a problem, Madame Caine? You don't care for your duckling?"

"She's just upset by the photographer," Dexter said. "Would you like something else, darling, or just the strawberries and champagne?"

Savannah shook her head. Being called "Madame Caine" seemed to have robbed her of the power of speech altogether.

"You don't need to worry about them disturbing you too much," Dexter added reassuringly—for the waiter's benefit, Savannah was certain. "I've got some plans to take care of that."

Savannah wasn't surprised. She also didn't think she was up to hearing about his plans just now—even if Dexter was in the mood to tell her. Which she doubted he was, considering how he'd been playing the game up till now.

She shook her head a little. "I just hope you've figured out how you're going to get us out of this mess."

"I'll work it out."

"That's what scares me."

He smiled. "Savannah, honey—have faith. That reminds me. I've been wondering why you have such an unusual name."

"I was named for the city I was born in," she said absently. "I was a little early, while my parents were on vacation in Georgia, and so...."

"It's very pretty."

"Thanks." She leaned forward and looked at him earnestly. "You know, Dexter, I've underestimated the difficulties of this situation. If we're going to be getting questions, it might not be a bad idea to have a few answers—ones we can actually agree on. For instance, how *did* we meet? I suppose I could have contacted you about ghostwriting your autobiography or something, but—"

"And though I wasn't interested in writing my life story, I *was* interested in getting to know you? It's not bad, really, as cover stories go. Still, it would be better not to answer any questions at all. Even a distant version of the truth gives them hints on where to start hunting, and complete fabrications are just too hard to remember."

"You sound like a man with experience in avoiding the facts," Savannah muttered. "Have you considered fiction as your next career?"

"Be careful, my dear. Just because we got rid of one camera doesn't mean they've all gone away."

The reminder stung a little, for she ought to have known better. "Of course. But I'm afraid it'll take me just a minute to get my look of adoration summoned up again."

Dexter laughed softly.

Raoul brought the strawberries, the huge slices of brilliant red fruit arranged artistically on a crystal plate and surrounded by a pale sauce of heavy cream and Cointreau. Dexter picked up Savannah's fork and fed the berries to her one by one.

At least, she told herself hopefully, there was a good chance he'd speeded things up tonight with that announcement. Perhaps it hadn't been such a ridiculous thing to say after all, now that she thought about it. If the tabloids really did take the bait and rush off chasing the phantom marriage license. . . .

Not a chance, she reminded herself. Tabloids simply didn't work that way, and if Dexter thought they'd be easy to lead around by the nose, he was apt to be disappointed.

Savannah had gotten hardly a glimpse of the casino area as they crossed the lobby earlier—she'd seen just enough to form an impression of noise and crowds and glitter. So she paused in the arched doorway to look around, while Dexter spoke to the security guard nearest the entrance.

She'd been right about the glitter; mirrors and crystal chandeliers and gold trim everywhere gave the place just a hint of the elegance of Versailles. But she'd been wrong about the crowds and the noise; though the room was comfortably full of people, it was so large it didn't look crammed, as she'd expected. And she was surprised to find that despite the throng the casino wasn't nearly as noisy as she'd expected, as well. A hundred or more slot machines ringed the room with a rhythmic clatter, punctuated by bells and buzzers. In the center of the room a pit boss was calling out some kind of code, and from hidden speakers in the ceiling, a public address system politely requested a customer to come to the hotel desk. Under it all was a gentle hum of conversation and the terse shorthand of gambling talk.

The security guard answered Dexter's question—which Savannah hadn't been listening to—and eyed her with what looked like suspicion.

Surely that wasn't his normal attitude when looking over a new patron, she thought, or no one would feel very welcome here. The hotel's grapevine must have already passed along the fascinating tale of what had happened in the restaurant.

Dexter took her arm. "Care to try your luck at blackjack?"

"No thanks," Savannah said sweetly. "Just hanging around with you is all the gamble I'm prepared to take tonight."

He laughed. "Then at least come and be my mascot." He sent a runner to the cashier's window for chips and took a seat at the nearest blackjack table.

Savannah stood close behind him, one hand resting on his shoulder in what she hoped was a cozy and intimate pose. The game moved with what seemed to her to be dizzying speed; she hadn't played blackjack in years, and then only for penny stakes. Before she could figure out what move would be best on Dexter's hand, not only he but the entire table had reacted, most of them with hand signals instead of words. Within a few minutes, Dexter won, and lost, then won again. The rhythm of the game was hypnotic, and Savannah moved a little closer yet, trying to read the signals.

He reached for her hand and drew it down across his chest till her palm rested against the starched front of his shirt just over his heart, and held it there, while he kept playing one-handed.

"Is this what you were doing last night?" she asked finally. "Playing blackjack till the wee hours of the morning?"

"Now, darling," Dexter murmured, without looking up from his cards. "Surely you aren't going to start out by being a nagging wife." The soft note in his voice was almost a caress.

The dealer shot an incredulous look at Savannah— she concluded that he hadn't yet heard the story—and almost knocked the cards off the table.

"But of course you're right that there are other forms of entertainment that are worthy of attention," Dexter murmured. He finished the hand and picked up his chips, pushing a few back toward the dealer as a tip. He waited till they were several yards from the table before adding crisply, "That should start the rumors going like wildfire in here."

"Happy to oblige," Savannah muttered. She wondered if the nagging-wife comment was part of his long-range plan. Perhaps he'd end up announcing that her henpecking had brought their happiness to a screeching halt, and imply that there was to be a divorce.

Not that it mattered, of course. She didn't much care how it all ended—as long as she could keep her name out of it so she'd still have a career when it was over.

"Is something wrong?" Dexter asked.

"Of course not," Savannah said with the merest hint of sarcasm. "I was dutifully admiring your brilliance. Not only have you fed the scandalmongers, but you're leaving with more cash than you had when you came in. What a perfect sting!"

"Yes. Isn't it marvelous? When I don't care whether I win, I hardly ever lose."

Nearby, a roulette wheel spun and clicked with machine-gun rapidity, slowing gradually as the ball bounced, then dropped into a numbered slot and stayed. Savannah paused to watch.

Dexter's eyebrows raised. "Is that your favorite?"

"If I was interested in gambling, which I'm not particularly," Savannah admitted, "roulette's the game that would fascinate me."

Dexter shook his head. "That's why casino owners adore people like you. Believe me, honey, the only person who wins at roulette is the one who owns the wheel."

"Isn't that true of the whole place? The house always wins."

"Over the course of time, yes. If there was no profit, there would be no casinos. But the odds for the player are better at some games than others, and roulette is certainly not a pastime for amateurs."

"You don't like it?"

"I'd rather spend my time with something that has an element of skill." He paused in the center of the lobby and looked down at her thoughtfully. "How about a nightcap in the bar?"

"And a little more gossip spreading?" She sighed. "I suppose, if it's really necessary—but I feel a little tipsy as it is."

"You should have eaten your duckling. I suppose we can quit for the night, if you'd rather. I think we've accomplished the main purpose, and going too far might cause questions."

At least a dozen people watched as he ushered her into the elevator with his arm draped ostentatiously around her shoulders. Savannah tried to ignore the onlookers. At least, to her relief, no one joined them for the ride.

As the elevator hummed toward the penthouse, she leaned against the wood-paneled wall with her eyes closed and said carelessly, "So you didn't win the hotel at roulette, then?"

Dexter didn't answer. Ultimately Savannah opened her eyes to find him shaking a gentle finger at her. "That was naughty. Did you really think I'd fall into that trap and tell you?"

Savannah shrugged. "You told me your strategy for winning."

"Oh, that's not a strategy, that's pure coincidence. Anybody could figure that out just from watching me for a while."

"So you still haven't really told me anything about you." Savannah knew she sounded frustrated.

Dexter smiled and ran his fingertip down the bridge of her nose. "You know what you have to do."

Inside the penthouse, only the wall sconces were lit, and they were turned down till not much more than a dim glow illuminated the living room. It was so quiet

and peaceful that Savannah wanted to kick off her shoes
and sink into the nearest couch.

"All in all, a successful evening, I'd say," Dexter said.
"Shall I roust out Robinson and have him make us a
pot of coffee?"

Savannah stared at him in amazement. "You'd really
bother him at this hour to make coffee? Are you completely helpless or what?"

"Is that another loaded question?"

Savannah put her hands on her hips. "You're a nasty,
distrustful sort, aren't you, Caine? Hasn't it occurred to
you that maybe I'd just like to know a little about you?
After all, if I'm going to be living with you for a
while—" She colored a little and hurried on. "Under
the same roof, at least. Of course I have a little personal
interest in you."

He looked interested. "You do?"

Savannah could have bitten her tongue off. "Not *that*
personal. I just meant I could be interested without in-
tending to publish anything at all." She saw the skeptical
lift of his brows and snapped, "All right. Do you have
a pen?" He produced one from the inside breast pocket
of his jacket with suspicious speed, and Savannah ripped
the top corner off the front page of the newspaper that
still lay on the sofa table. "Maybe you'd better speak
to Robinson after all," she muttered. "Leaving the place
cluttered up like this...."

She scribbled a sentence in the white margin, signed
her name with a flourish, and thrust the scrap of paper
at him.

Dexter turned it to the light and read, "I promise I
will not publish any information given me by Dexter
Caine without his prior permission."

"It's not notarized," she snapped, "but it ought to
do."

Dexter looked from the paper to her face. "Yes, it'll
do." He folded the note tenderly and slipped it into his

breast pocket. "This is a promise I'll always hold close to my heart, Savannah," he murmured.

The note of laughter in his voice made Savannah want to scream. "I bet you will."

"So what do you want to ask me about first?"

Questions bubbled through her mind. How had he got his start? Did he think he had some sort of magic touch with investments? Why did his factories seem endlessly profitable when others—sometimes in the same industries—struggled to stay afloat? How and why did he suddenly own a hotel in Las Vegas, and what was he really going to do with it?

Then Savannah remembered the humor in his voice, and realized that a quick, eager interrogation was precisely what he expected. She had no doubt he'd enjoy it, too—and she suspected darkly that despite her promise he'd tell her precisely as much as he wanted her to know and not one word more.

Well, she was in no mood to be toyed with. She raised her chin and said, "I have just one question, really."

"Only one? You amaze me, Savannah."

"Am I allowed to use the telephone? I check in with my mother every Sunday morning, you see, and she'll be worried if I don't call."

Blank astonishment filled his eyes. "*That's* what you want to know?"

"At the moment, it's by far the most important question on my mind. What good could it possibly do me to spend the night listening to stories about you when I can't use them?" There, she thought. That should put him properly in his place. Though she hadn't exactly said she expected his stories to be boring—the kind she'd only put up with for the sake of selling the information—she thought the implication was clear enough.

The corner of Dexter's mouth quirked. "Your mother doesn't work for Associated Press, does she?"

"My mother is a dear little lady who lives in Urbana, Illinois, makes quilts with her church group, and takes casseroles to what she calls the elderly—some of whom are younger than she is."

The quirk had become a full-fledged grin. "Not the kind of person you'd like to disappoint."

"No. She's a world champion when it comes to producing guilt."

"She reminds me of my grandmother," Dexter said. "Ask Robinson in the morning and he'll find you a phone. If you don't want coffee—"

"That's the last thing I need."

"Then I'll say good-night."

Savannah realized too late that she wanted to ask him about his grandmother—but the dismissal in his voice had been unmistakable. She turned toward the bedroom wing. It was silly to feel as if she was being sent to her room; she was still overwrought from the pressures of the evening, that was all.

"Savannah." His quiet voice called her back. "The necklace, please."

Her hand went to the band of diamonds at her throat. How quickly she'd gotten used to the weight and the feel of the stones. She fumbled with the clasp and dropped the necklace into his outstretched hand. The gold was warm from her skin.

She unfastened the earrings and laid them on his palm. "Thanks for the loan," she said. "I'll probably never wear anything so beautiful again." She caught what sounded like a tiny tinge of self-pity in her voice; she hoped he hadn't heard it. "Unless of course you've got something even better for tomorrow," she added in a lighter tone.

Dexter shook his head. "Not likely." The flat note in his voice made it clear that the question of jewelry was less than important to him.

Savannah forced a smile. "Good night."

She was far too tense to relax; even the soothing steps of her regular nightly routine didn't help. She put on the pajamas the boutique had sent, though she shook her head in surprise. They were tailored, all right, just as she'd requested. They were also made of the softest, sheerest satin Savannah had ever encountered.

Her computer was still set up on the table by the French doors, and she turned it on. She might as well do a little work; that was guaranteed to help her unwind. Maybe she should work on her half-finished article about the aftereffects of physical abuse of women. In its present form it was dull enough to send her off to sleep—which didn't sound so bad at the moment. There was also her article on hospice care that still lacked a bit of polishing before it could be sent off....

But she didn't pull up either of those files. Instead, she called up the *Today's Woman* piece on Dexter Caine. It was still a good story, she thought, but now she could see shadowy holes here and there where something was lacking. Some vital bit of information that only Dexter knew, which would flesh out the picture of this incredibly interesting man.

There was so much more to tell. There were dimensions to Dexter Caine that no one had ever explored, far more than could be tackled in any mere magazine piece. It would take a book—a big book—to do justice to him. A major biography.

But there was no sense even in thinking about that. Dexter would never go along with anything of the sort, and so long as he held her promise, Savannah couldn't write a word of it.

"Actually," she murmured to herself, "I can *write* whatever I please. What I said was that I wouldn't *publish* it."

It was a fine distinction, however, and one that made no difference whatsoever. Still, there was nothing wrong with dreaming.

She opened a new file and started listing the questions she'd like to ask Dexter Caine. It was a lengthy list, and an hour slid by unnoticed before a dull ache in the pit of her stomach reminded her that strawberries—even drenched in that rich and wonderful sauce—hardly made an adequate dinner. Dexter was right; she should have eaten her duckling.

Surely somewhere in Robinson's kitchen she could find something to nibble on. And if she was very quiet, she wouldn't disturb anyone else.

The sconces still gleamed in the living room. Savannah made a mental note to add a question to her list—was there a reason Dexter liked to have night-lights glowing all the time? Then she heard soft, slow, relaxed breathing, and realized she wasn't alone.

Dexter was sprawled on the couch with one foot on the cushions, the other on the floor. He'd taken his jacket off, and his tie and the collar of his formal shirt were loose. On his chest lay an open book, as if he'd laid it down to rest his eyes a moment and unexpectedly gone to sleep. Savannah noted the dust jacket with astonishment; the last thing she'd have expected Dexter Caine to be reading was a thriller called *The Twelve Days of Murder*.

And despite the fact that his clothes were rumpled and his hair was standing straight on end, he was still extraordinarily handsome.

She hadn't noticed the reading lamp beside the couch when she first came into the room because its black shade forced all the light down onto the page—or in this case, directly onto Dexter's face. It was the first time she'd been able to truly look without his being aware of her scrutiny, and she took advantage of the opportunity.

She hadn't noticed before how long his lashes were; the strong light cast incredible shadows across his cheekbones. His eyebrows no longer had the cynical tilt she'd been growing so accustomed to seeing; they'd relaxed into a natural aristocratic arch. His hair looked silky....

Her fingers itched a little to smooth a soft curl back from his temple. *Oh, that's just what we need*, she told herself. If he woke up and found her here in her pajamas, after what had happened last night...

She wouldn't mind a bit if he did wake up and find her leaning over him. And after that...she wasn't sure she'd mind, no matter what he did.

The confession rocked her a little, but there was no denying it was the truth. That was why her whole body had tingled this morning as she'd modeled clothes for him, feeling as if he could look straight through the fabric if he'd half tried. Even in the midst of their quarrels, she'd felt alive, and eager, and aware—oh, so aware—of his vitality, his virility. Dexter Caine was one fascinating, exciting male, and Savannah had—for all practical purposes—been tossed straight into his arms.

And now she was in real danger of losing her head. She was standing in the middle of his living room wearing a pair of tailored satin pajamas, which suddenly felt very sexy indeed, and hoping he'd wake up and find her there, just so she could see what would happen.

Savannah Seabrooke, she told herself, you're losing your mind.

He didn't move, and his breathing relaxed slowly into a tiny snore. After a moment, common sense reasserted itself and Savannah went back to her room. Funny, she thought, that she didn't seem to feel hungry anymore.

For food, at least.

Robinson was just arranging a carafe of coffee over a warming candle on the sideboard when Savannah came into the room the next morning. Dexter was nowhere to be seen; Savannah told herself it was silly to feel even an instant's letdown. He was a busy man after all.

"Good morning, miss," Robinson said, and Savannah wondered if he hadn't yet heard the rumors, or if he'd been told the story of the supposed marriage and simply didn't believe it because of what he'd been overhearing around the suite, or if Dexter had confided at least part of the truth. There wasn't any point in trying to figure it out from the butler's expression, however, she decided. The fleeting moments of embarrassment he'd felt yesterday seemed to have been put firmly in the past.

Three major newspapers were arranged neatly on the dining table, and Robinson unwrapped a napkin from a basket of golden pastries while Savannah poured herself a cup of coffee.

"What a gold mine," she said happily. "Coffee and croissants and *three* newspapers...." The front page of the *New York Times* was warm to her touch. "I suppose you ironed all of these? Robinson, you're compulsive."

"It is my responsibility to make things comfortable, miss."

"Oh, don't try to come over stuffy on me. The truth is you're just a dear, and you like doing things to please people. Does anyone call you anything but Robinson?"

"No, miss."

"I'm surprised. You act more like a Robbie sometimes." She laughed merrily at the shock that rippled across his face.

Savannah put a napkin and a croissant atop the *Times* and carried the newspaper and her coffee to the living-room area, where she settled cross-legged in the middle of the deep-piled geometric rug. "By the way, Robinson, Mr. Caine kindly gave me permission to use the telephone this morning, but since I haven't seen one in the whole suite yet...."

He looked a little less than convinced.

"Oh, by all means ask him when he comes back," Savannah said kindly. "Though I hope he hasn't gone too far—it's only going to be morning in Illinois for a couple more hours.'' She buried her nose in the editorial section.

"Where do you think I'd have gone anyway?'' Dexter asked.

Savannah looked up so fast that her neck snapped. He was standing less than a yard from her, and from her perspective he looked about nine feet tall. He was wearing dark, easy-fitting trousers and a cotton sweater over an open-necked shirt; the diamond pattern knitted into the sweater added breadth to his shoulders and made him even more formidable than usual. And just as handsome....

"You sneaked up on me,'' Savannah accused. She felt just a little breathless, and she was annoyed at herself for forgetting that this wasn't a relationship but a one-act play.

"Would you like me to wear a bell, like a cat?''

She smiled suddenly. "I'm sure the tabloid people would appreciate that.''

She hadn't seen him give Robinson any signal, but the butler returned with a telephone. He set it down on the rug beside her and plugged the long cord into a well-hidden jack in the wall.

Savannah supposed she shouldn't be terribly surprised that she wasn't to be allowed any privacy to make her call. If she'd been in Dexter Caine's shoes, she'd probably have insisted—promise or no promise—on checking to be sure the person on the other end of the line really was a dear old mother and not a newspaper copydesk somewhere. But Dexter seemed unconcerned. In fact, he disappeared into the kitchen, following Robinson.

Maybe he wants to learn to make coffee, Savannah thought. She toyed with the telephone while she considered how much to tell her mother. The trouble was, there could be no easy or partial explanation; it was either the whole truth or nothing at all. She sighed. It wouldn't be the first time she'd tried to keep Connie Seabrooke in the dark—something which was more easily said than done.

Savannah braced herself and dialed, and mere moments later her mother answered. "Were you sitting beside the phone again, Mother?"

"Well, it's getting a bit late. You usually call earlier than this. Did you have a nice long date last night or something?"

That description didn't begin to touch the evening she'd had, Savannah thought. "You could say that, I suppose. Pretty nice anyway."

"Have I met him? Or will I, soon?"

"Very doubtful. Look, Mother, would you call Jack and give him a message from me?"

"Why, darling? Aren't you at home?"

"No. I'm sort of on assignment."

"Oh? Have you taken a more regular kind of job?" Connie's voice was hopeful.

Not by a long shot, Savannah thought. "No, this is a temporary kind of thing. If you'd just call Jack and ask him to water my plants till I get back—"

Dexter had wandered back into the room. "Who's Jack?"

Connie said, "Savannah, do you have a man in your apartment?"

"Would you hush?" Savannah hissed at Dexter and turned back to the phone. "No, Mother."

"Oh, that's right, you're not even in your apartment. Then where are you?"

Savannah decided the best way to avoid that question was to ignore it and go on the offensive. "In any case, if I did have a man in my apartment, it wouldn't be the first time and it doesn't mean a thing. Having a man in one's apartment on a Sunday morning doesn't mean he spent Saturday night there, too."

"That's a shame," Connie said calmly. "Depending on the man, of course."

"Who's Jack?" Dexter persisted.

Obviously he wasn't going to give up. "My landlord," Savannah muttered.

"I *know* he's your landlord," Connie said. "Very well, I'll ask Jack to water your plants. Anything else?"

"Yes. Tell him I'll take care of everything as soon as I get home. Emphasize the 'everything', okay?" With Dexter standing right there listening to every word, she could hardly tell her mother about her rent being late. Besides, Connie would have a fit and probably give Savannah yet another lecture about the value of a regular job with a stable employer. "Sorry I can't talk longer, Mom, but I'll check in again next weekend, all right?" She put the telephone down with a grateful sigh.

"Your landlord actually waters plants?" Dexter asked. "What kind of arrangement do you have anyway?"

Savannah sighed. "It's a brownstone. Jack lives in the main apartment and rents out the other three. We all look after each other's stuff. I walk Jack's dog, he waters my plants.... It's a fair trade-off."

He sat down at the end of the couch. "Why didn't you tell your mother where you are?"

"Because I've got enough trouble without trying to explain all this to my mother."

"What do you plan to do when she sees your face on the front page of the tabloids next week?"

"Maybe the pictures will be blurry," Savannah said. Or maybe Connie would break a leg and have to stay home till after the whole episode had played itself out. Of course, even that wouldn't help much; Connie's friends would no doubt keep her informed.

Savannah pushed herself up from the rug and went to get her reading glasses so she could bury herself in the newspapers for the rest of the morning, or at least until Dexter's next brainstorm.

She stopped dead in the doorway of her room at the sight of Robinson bending over the foot of her bed, carefully laying clothes into a suitcase. Savannah hadn't even seen him go down the hall toward her room, but he'd obviously been at work for a while; the closet doors were open and empty hangers occupied the space that just this morning had held rows of beautiful clothes.

But there hadn't even been time for the story to hit the papers yet, she thought frantically. Surely Dexter wouldn't send her away now, before he could be certain his campaign was successful!

Though on the other hand, he'd said last night he was impatient for results, and when she'd given back the necklace with the halfhearted joke about an even more beautiful one to wear today, he'd dismissed the idea very coolly.

Still, if all he'd intended was one evening, one appearance, why had he bought all the clothes? Had he intended them as some sort of bonus? But he'd also said she'd need them all. Had he changed his mind last night? This morning? Was it something she'd said or done?

She put her fingertips to her temples. She was starting to sound as if this was real—as if she had the power to upset him enough to make him want to send her away!

"Robinson, what are you doing?" she said. Her voice was shrill, and she stopped to clear her throat and reconsider. If she was to be dismissed, she could at least keep her dignity intact. "Sorry, I didn't realize I was going home just yet. Don't pack those things—they aren't mine. I'll just take what I came with."

Robinson's hands didn't pause. "You'll need them in Winter Park, miss."

"*Where?*"

Suddenly she felt the warmth of a body close behind her, and a tendril of her hair stirred as Dexter said, almost in her ear, "Winter Park, Colorado. It's a ski resort, and since it's out of season it will be very private. Don't you think it's only sensible that we'd slip off to a little hideaway somewhere to be completely alone, my darling?''

CHAPTER SIX

THE idea of their slipping off to some isolated mountain hideaway to be alone did make sense. That was one of the things that scared Savannah.

I'm beginning to think like Dexter Caine, she told herself in despair, but she didn't have time to wonder why that fact bothered her so much.

Dexter said, "Robinson will leave out the dress I want you to wear."

"Oh, now you've taken to dictating everything I put on, too? What's wrong with what I've chosen?" Savannah's gesture took in her loosely fitted periwinkle trousers and coordinating blouse. "You seemed to like these things yesterday."

"Nothing's wrong, but for this occasion I think we need something a little more dramatic." He stepped past her and pushed the closet door open a little farther. "Yes, this will be just right."

Savannah eyed the red dress that was the only thing still hanging in her closet and the matching wide-brimmed hat that was perched on the shelf just above. "That's the one thing you bought yesterday that I really hate, Dexter."

"Oh? Why?"

Savannah made a face. Her distaste was hard to explain, for the fabric was beautiful, the cut was excellent, the fit superb. Even the color—not just red, but a sharp watermelon red—had looked good on her, despite her initial hesitation about wearing anything in that shade. It was just that there was so very much red, and not even a contrasting accent to break it up.

"It's so eye-catching," she said.

"I know. That's why I want you to wear it today." Dexter picked up the hat and set it on her head. "With the veil just slightly over your eyes, like so."

Savannah looked up at him through the red mist formed by the delicate net veil. "If this hat was green instead of red, I'd look like a walking tomato," she muttered.

Dexter's gaze skimmed her figure as if for the first time. "No, you wouldn't."

A warm and delicious sensation spiraled up from the pit of Savannah's stomach.

Then he added calmly, "To the best of my knowledge, there's never been a tomato that was shaped anything like you."

She stuck her tongue out at him. He laughed and went on down the hall to his own room.

This time they left the hotel through the front entrance. Dexter had changed into a dark suit; the narrow stripe in his tie matched the shade of Savannah's dress. It was a very subtle statement of togetherness, though Savannah thought it would probably be wasted on the tabloid types, who tended to think in broader terms. She didn't bother to tell Dexter that, however.

The limousine that had brought her from the airport was waiting under the canopied front entrance, and the driver stood at attention beside the open passenger door. Savannah wondered how long he'd been standing there.

Dexter paused to greet him, dallying—Savannah was certain—for the benefit of the cameras pointed at them. She wondered how many of them belonged to tourists and how many were stakeouts from the tabloids.

She stood on her toes so she could whisper into Dexter's ear. "Won't they notice how unusual it is for you to be cooperative?"

"Probably." He slipped an arm around her waist to steady her, and smiled down into her eyes. Nearby, a fcmale tourist released a gusty sigh of envy. Dexter paid no attention. "But then it's highly unusual for me to be showing off a sexy lady in red, too. You'll no doubt get the credit for bringing me around."

Savannah could imagine it. *Mystery Wife Tames Dexter Caine.* Now that was just what she didn't need.

Dexter looked around for Robinson, who hurried up carrying a large flat white box. "This was just delivered, sir," he said, loud enough for the crowd to hear.

Dexter took the box and held it out to Savannah. "You'll need this in the mountains, darling."

The crowd, which had gotten larger, pushed a little closer.

Savannah stared at him in disbelief and said, her lips barely moving, "You expect me to open this right here? Now?"

Dexter's eyebrows went up just a fraction. "Of course."

"I know. Any woman you'd be seriously interested in couldn't wait to drool over a gift."

He was still holding the box as she lifted the lid.

There was nothing premeditated about Savannah's gasp; no woman could have looked down on a double armful of rich, glossy dark mink and not reacted. But the gaze she raised to his was full of dismay.

"It's borrowed," he said under his breath.

Savannah stood on her toes again and let her lips brush his cheek in what she hoped looked like a fond thank-you. She tried to ignore the tingle that leaped from his skin to hers and rocketed through her every nerve. "I assumed that much," she muttered. "But I don't care if it *is* borrowed. I don't wear fur."

Dexter didn't seem to hear. "I'm so glad you like it," he said clearly. "It's just a little thing, really."

The crowd murmured and shifted in obvious disagreement.

"But if you'd like to express your appreciation properly, my dear...." He took the lid out of her hands and handed the box to the chauffeur, who stood stiffly as if wondering what he was supposed to do with it.

Dexter put both arms around Savannah and drew her even closer. She had only an instant to brace herself for the impact of his kiss, before he took her lips with what must have looked like the easy confidence of a man who knows his embrace is welcomed.

Every woman in the crowd sighed.

They're all picturing themselves in my shoes, Savannah thought. Well, she'd happily trade places—but the only thing she could do at the moment was to sink against him in surrender and remind herself that she was only playing a part and she didn't enjoy being put on display like this....

A soft little tingle of satisfaction started deep in the pit of her stomach, and the longer Dexter kissed her, the farther the sensation spread. She felt as if warm honey was oozing through every vein.

She arched her neck to press her mouth more tightly against his, and though she felt her hat begin to slide, she didn't bother to reach for it. Dexter had quicker reflexes; he caught the hat and pressed it back into place. He looked down at her with a sultry smile and whispered, "Sorry, darling. I'm afraid I got a little carried away."

He sounded so convincing that for a split second Savannah wondered if he actually meant it. Then she saw a tinge of puzzlement creep into his eyes—as if he was wondering why she was looking at him so intently—and she blinked and turned her head, reminding herself that she was dealing with a Broadway-caliber actor. If Dexter had really been carried away, he wouldn't have cared any more about her hat falling off than she had.

But of course she had cared, she added hastily. She'd simply been throwing herself into her part, pretending she didn't.

Dexter helped her into the car, and as soon as the door was closed, she moved to the far side and sat up stiffly, knowing that the darkened windows prevented the crowd outside from seeing even a silhouette. Robinson took the box full of mink and climbed into the front with the chauffeur, and the limousine pulled slowly away. Dexter leaned back in the corner of the deep leather seat and looked at her thoughtfully.

Savannah straightened her hat and dug a tiny mirror out of her handbag so she could check her lipstick. "Good performance," she said crisply. "The stage lost a tremendous star when you decided to go into business."

"Thank you." Dexter's voice was slow and easy. "You're something of a champion yourself."

She paused with a lipstick brush in her hand, wondering if there might be a hidden message somewhere in that, and decided that he only meant he wasn't disappointed in ending up with her playing this part instead of Muffy—or whatever the woman's name was. She snapped the mirror shut and thrust it back into her handbag. "Do I get a bonus?"

Dexter smiled. "Depends. What have you got in mind?"

"I'll think it over and let you know." She tugged at the bottom of her skirt and made a mental note for the future—she'd sit down whenever she was trying on clothes, just to be sure she could. This particular dress was cut so that there was no keeping the hem in place, particularly in a soft, deeply cushioned seat.

Dexter hadn't missed the maneuver, and Savannah was surprised when he didn't say anything. Instead, he turned to look out the back window of the limousine for a last view of the hotel as they drew away into the empty desert toward the airport.

"Aren't you expecting to see it again?" she asked.

"What? Of course I am." He settled back in his seat again. "Are you still convinced I'm going to tear it down and build something odd? Maybe a Mayan high temple complete with virgin sacrifices?"

"Oh, no," Savannah murmured. "You couldn't possibly find an adequate supply of virgins for three shows a day."

Dexter laughed. "That might be a problem, come to think of it. Which reminds me, you said something to your mother this morning about having men stay over at your apartment. Is there one in particular I should know about, or is this only a now-and-then sort of thing?"

Savannah stared at him. "Now if that isn't a loaded question, I have never heard one. No matter how I answer it, I come off looking cheap."

"I just meant—"

"It's obvious what you meant! No, there is no one in particular, and no, I'm not in the habit of letting anyone stay overnight, even now and then. Is that clear enough or shall I take it from the top?"

"But you did tell your mother...."

"What I told my mother was that a morning guest wasn't necessarily an overnight one, too," she reminded him.

"So you did. Of course, I'd expect you to tell her that. You wouldn't want to shock a sweet little lady who quilts and does charity work...."

"If you think she'd be shocked, you obviously don't understand mothers. She used to nag me about getting married, but for the past couple of years she's just been saying wistfully that she's not getting any younger and she'd like to have some grandchildren." Savannah gave her hem another impatient tug.

Dexter's gaze drifted to her knees, and stayed.

Savannah said, "But that can't possibly interest you. Besides, you're dodging *my* question about the hotel."

For a moment she thought he was going to ignore her. Of course, that would be nothing new.

Then he said slowly, "You're right about the land being a gold mine, and if anyone is crazy enough to pay me what it's worth, I'd no doubt sell. But in the meantime . . . well, let's just say Mayan high temples and re-creations of Mars aren't my idea of a good investment."

"Then you're not planning to tear the hotel down?"

"No. I'm convinced that in the long run, elegance and quality and service will outlast all the hoopla."

Savannah frowned. "But you'd consider selling it? I don't understand."

"You see, Savannah, each new resort in this town has to make its cost back quickly before the next new one comes along to steal its thunder—which in itself is becoming increasingly difficult, since every year it takes more to astound a jaded public. Maybe you hit the jackpot, maybe you lose your shirt. I'd rather not gamble on those odds. I'll settle for a slow and steady return, with little risk, while I wait for someone to come along who wants to roll the dice on that piece of land."

The car slid to a halt so smoothly that for a moment Savannah didn't realize they had arrived. She was caught up in Dexter's reasoning, absorbed in his philosophy. It made sense, yet there was something about it that simply didn't fit.

The chauffeur opened the door. She saw that Robinson was already climbing aboard the little plane, the box full of mink in his arms.

"We might as well not take that coat," she said. "I'm not wearing it."

"Even in September, it gets chilly in the Rockies. You may change your mind."

Savannah shrugged. "I doubt it, but if taking it along will make you happy, have your own way."

Dexter's eyes glinted. "I generally do. What's the big deal about fur anyway? You're wearing snakeskin shoes right now."

She looked down at her high-heeled red pumps. "That's not quite the same thing."

"It certainly is. Unless you're basing your philosophy on the fond belief that snakes aren't cuddly and minks are—in which case you're sadly wrong."

Her eyes widened. "You don't mean you *like* snakes?"

"Any reason I shouldn't? More than I like mink, at any rate. Those little animals are vicious."

Savannah shivered delicately. "I suppose you had snakes when you were a kid?"

"What makes you think I don't own a few now?"

Savannah stared at him. The light in his eyes was simple mischief—wasn't it? In any case, even if the man raised pythons, there wasn't much she could do about it.

Two crewmen began to unload the luggage from the limousine's trunk and transfer it to the cargo compartment in the plane's belly.

Savannah spotted her tote bag just as one of the crewmen started to stow it away with the rest of the bags. She retrieved it, and Dexter carried it on board. "You won't have time to do much," he said. "The flight should be less than two hours."

"I just feel better when I have my computer handy."

"Even when you don't have anything to write about?"

"Who said I don't have anything to write about? You surely don't think you're the only subject on my mind."

Dexter winced. "That puts me properly in my place." He stashed the bag in a small compartment and waved a hand at the assortment of seats. "Take your choice."

Savannah noticed that though the box containing the mink jacket had been placed on one of the forward seats, the butler was nowhere in sight. "Isn't Robinson coming with us?"

Dexter looked around as if he hadn't noticed. "Oh, he's probably in the galley." He pointed to a tiny door Savannah had assumed was just another storage compartment.

"There's a kitchen on board this thing?"

"Well, it wasn't part of the original design. But I enjoy my creature comforts, so we fit it in. The best thing that can be said for it is that it's efficient."

"I'd say it would have to be. What's he doing? Whipping up a gourmet meal to keep us entertained for an hour in the air?"

"Of course not. He just likes his privacy."

"I'll bet," Savannah murmured. Being invisible when one wasn't needed seemed to be an unspoken rule of working for Dexter Caine.

She felt the cargo door slam beneath her feet, and soon the engines began to vibrate. She selected a seat, and Dexter sat down across from her and pulled his seat belt tight.

The plane rolled slowly down the taxiway, and Dexter reached into a drawer and pulled out a box of assorted chocolates. Savannah shook her head when he offered it to her.

He selected a raspberry cream and asked lazily, "Why are you frowning? Surely you're not still afraid to fly?"

"Who told you I was?" She unpinned her hat and laid it carefully on the table between them.

"The crew."

"Oh." And when had they had the opportunity to confide that? she wondered. "I wasn't afraid."

"Pity," Dexter murmured. "There are all sorts of fun ways to overcome a fear of flying."

Savannah knew better than to ask what he had in mind. "I was just upset to find I was going to Las Vegas, when I really only intended to ask you a couple of questions and then hop off the plane.''

"You were disappointed that I wasn't aboard? What a shame. If I'd known—''

"You'd have made a point of being there? Too bad you didn't. It would have saved me a lot of trouble.'' The runway sped by in a blur, and then the city fell away below them. Savannah watched it shrink into a toy-size panorama and then disappear as they left the desert bowl and climbed over the mountains, and wondered why she had such an all-gone feeling in her stomach. It must be the speed of the plane's ascent, she decided. It certainly couldn't be regret at leaving Las Vegas.

Dexter smiled a little. "Anyway, if it's not flying that's been bothering you, why were you frowning? Because you've got a tidbit about me that you can't use?''

Savannah shook her head. "No, it's the hotel. I don't understand your caution, Dexter. It's not that I don't follow your reasoning. In fact, it makes perfect sense to me, but....''

He poked through the chocolate box. "Then what's the problem?''

"But that can't be the way you made your money. You must have taken enormous chances along the way. So why would you be so cautious now?''

"Of course I've taken chances. I still do—but I do it in areas where I have a bit of skill.''

She thought that over. "Like playing blackjack instead of roulette?''

"Exactly. I'd rather bet on myself than trust raw luck, which is what I'd be doing if I took a flyer and built a resort.''

"So how *did* you get that hotel? And why?''

"Because it's a good piece of land, and I took it in exchange for a very bad, very overdue debt. So you see, you were right about that, too. A casino *is* a strange thing for me to own.'' He stretched out his legs. "You know, this business of being interviewed is downright interesting, Savannah. Any other questions you'd like answered?''

"You're only telling me all this because I've promised not to use what you say, aren't you?"

"Of course. You wouldn't expect me to tell you anything if you hadn't promised, would you?"

"I've a good mind not to talk to you anymore," Savannah said coolly. "Even if I'd later get the same information somewhere else, I couldn't use it because you'd say I got it from you."

"Really?" His voice was innocent. "Is that the way the rules work?"

She looked daggers at him.

"Have it your own way, though," he murmured. "If you don't want to talk about me, then tell me about you. What have you done for fun on the job besides slog through waste dumps?"

Well, that little gambit had gotten her nowhere, she thought. And they still had a couple of hours to kill. "I covered the police beat in a small city once."

"Oh, that sounds exciting."

"It wasn't. Mostly it was car accidents and drunk drivers—but I still had to be on call all the time in case something important turned up. Long hours and low pay...." Her eyes narrowed. "In fact, it was a little like this job."

"Oh, not at all. On this job, you have the indignity of wearing mink," Dexter said mildly.

She raised her chin. "Try to make me."

"Don't issue challenges unless you're prepared for them to be taken up, Savannah."

His voice was smooth and lazy. She told herself it was only her own imagination that found a note of warning underneath.

"What were the questions you wanted to ask?" he added.

A bit uneasily, she remembered the list safely stored in her computer's memory. But Dexter couldn't know about those. "What do you mean?"

"You said you intended to ask me a couple of questions and then hop off the plane."

"Oh, that. The questions don't matter anymore. You've answered the most important one anyway."

"How I got the hotel?"

"No." She hesitated, and then decided there was no reason not to talk about it. "Didn't I tell you? I wanted to know about Cassie King."

"You disappoint me. So you were just another member of the crowd that's been shouting, 'When's the wedding?' whenever they can get within range?"

"Of course not. I knew the real story was that there wouldn't be a wedding. I just wanted you to confirm it."

He looked at her so long and so intently that Savannah began to squirm.

"What's the matter?" she asked finally.

"How did you know that?"

She shrugged. "Remember a couple of years ago on that talk show when Cassie modestly admitted she'd once saved a woman's life before a concert?"

Dexter shook his head. "I never pay attention to talk shows. They're no closer to reality than the tabloids are, and I think they both deserve to be—" He stopped, as if he'd said a little more than he intended.

"So you *are* doing this on purpose to get even with the press." Savannah tried to keep the triumph she felt from coming through in her voice. Her brainstorm that first morning had been right on the money after all!

Dexter leaned back in his seat and smiled. "Don't tell me you're shocked. Cassie's publicity stunts are a nuisance, and she's been told several times to cut it out, without any success. But I must admit that what really tickled my sense of humor about this particular scheme was the idea of leading the tabloids down the garden path.''

"You could just sue them."

"But that's so useless, you see—it only gives them more to talk about. This way, *I* get to choose the subject—and the real beauty of it is they'll probably never realize they've been had."

"Secret revenge?"

"It's the most satisfying sort, my dear—at least with opponents like these. Now what was that story about Cassie and the woman she saved?"

Savannah wasn't quite satisfied, but it was apparent he'd said all he was going to. "Well, I did some asking around, and I found someone who was there. The woman had a heart attack, all right, but Cassie was no help. In fact, the paramedics had to revive her after she fainted in horror."

"I don't quite see what that's got to do with me."

"It's not the only time that Cassie's stories have turned out not to have happened quite the way she told them. I thought it was likely this was another, because if you wanted to marry her you'd have done it a long time ago."

"Maybe she was too devoted to her career."

"The career you started by introducing her to the head of the record company?" Savannah shook her head. "I doubt that would have stopped you."

"You're scary, Savannah."

"So I'm right?"

"I didn't stay that. But I'm beginning to be very glad I've got you safely under my thumb instead of still out there somewhere wildly speculating."

"Who says I've stopped speculating just because I'm here? Maybe when this is over I'll call up Cassie King. I never promised not to write *her* biography, and look at the background material I'm getting."

He smiled slowly. "I'll introduce you."

So much for that threat, Savannah thought. She asked in a practical tone, "How? She's not going to be speaking to you for the next hundred years."

"I guess that is a problem, isn't it?" It didn't seem to bother him.

Savannah had never seen the Rockies from the air; her only cross-country flights had been at higher altitudes on cloudy days. So for much of the last half of the flight, she kept her nose pressed against the window, admiring the rough, craggy peaks, the green swatches of valleys, even the winding gray ribbons of the roads that meandered around the mountains.

She was only half-aware of Dexter watching her. "Have you never seen the mountains before?" he asked finally.

She refused to be embarrassed by the amusement in his voice. "Not since I was a kid. And never like this." She didn't turn from the window.

"It's a long way from south Chicago." His tone was no longer amused; it was understanding.

"In more ways than one," she said, and wondered if Dexter had made that journey himself. Had his beginnings been humble? Or had he built on the resources of a family? She was relatively sure he hadn't started with wealth, for surely a family fortune would have come to light in the course of her research. But that didn't mean he had been penniless.

Before she could frame the question, Dexter added, "Then you're in for a treat. In many ways the Rockies are as beautiful as the Alps." He moved across to sit beside her. His arm came to rest gently around her shoulders as he leaned forward to point out the landmarks. His warmth and strength surrounded her like the faint essence of his cologne.

Savannah felt a sudden almost overwhelming desire to lean back against him, cushioning the hard angles of his body with her own soft curves, and she had to tug herself back to reality.

The soft wool of his sleeve brushed her cheek as he showed her the way early snow had dusted the side of a mountaintop below them. It looked like confectioners' sugar, spread slapdash across a cake, but he said in places it was probably several feet thick.

"What happens if you get snowbound?" she asked.

"I never have been. Or at least I've never noticed."

She tipped her head back and looked over her shoulder at him. His eyes had a faraway look while he gazed out over the rugged peaks, as if he drew strength from the sight.

"That sounds strange, doesn't it?" he said. "I run my businesses by phone and fax most of the time anyway, so wherever I am, weather doesn't keep me from doing my work. Besides, I like snow."

"Why are we going to Winter Park in particular? Why not Aspen or Vail? They're much better known."

Dexter smiled. "That's exactly why. Winter Park is one of the few places where I can just be myself."

And who are you? Savannah thought.

He had turned his attention back to the scenery, and she thought he was probably unaware that his cheek had come to rest against her hair. No doubt from that angle he had a better view through the tiny window.

She sat very still, trying not to breathe, trying not to disturb the mood. Once—just a couple of days ago, in fact—she had thought she knew a great deal about Dexter Caine. Now she understood that there was a whole lot of difference between having information and truly knowing a person. Now she believed a lifetime wouldn't be enough to find out who he was....

But of course, she didn't have a lifetime to research Dexter Caine. And a fortunate thing it was, too, she told herself rather tartly. What on earth would she do with all that knowledge if she couldn't write about him?

There was an ache in the pit of her stomach. Savannah tried to ignore it. "You spend a lot of time here, then?"

"Whenever I can manage it. These mountains are one of my favorite places in the world." The pitch of the engines changed subtly. "Look—there's the landing strip."

"Landing strip?" Savannah could see a narrow little ribbon of concrete in the distance. "You mean there's not even an airport?"

"I don't need a whole airport," he said patiently. "So why build one?"

"You own the airstrip?" Savannah didn't know why she should be surprised. She obviously was going to have to adjust her thinking; she'd assumed they'd stay at one of the resort hotels. She supposed she should have expected when he'd mentioned a hideaway that he'd have a condo; not only would it be more private, but it would be ready at a moment's notice whenever he wanted it.

"Driving out from Denver every time I want to spend a few days here is hardly my idea of fun. And I don't like helicopters. Don't ask me why. I can't explain it." He moved back into his original seat and fastened his safety belt. "So building the airstrip was the best alternative."

The sudden emptiness at her back left Savannah feeling cold.

There were two vehicles waiting at the end of the concrete runway where the plane eventually drew up; one was a small dark blue sports car, the other a Jeep. Crewmen immediately started unloading the bags from the cargo bay into the Jeep. Dexter ignored them and led the way to the sports car.

"No media?" Savannah asked.

"Are you missing them already? Don't worry. It'll take just a little while for them to catch up. That's another advantage of private airstrips, you see. Even if they were here already, they couldn't come onto private property and annoy us.''

Dexter had been right about the mountain air being chilly; even in the little meadow the sunshine somehow didn't seem to penetrate. Savannah shivered, then remembered the mink jacket and decided that she'd rather not explain to Dexter again why she'd prefer being cold to wearing it. So she firmly subdued the shiver.

The car was warm, though, and she relaxed and enjoyed the view. The meadow soon vanished behind them as the valley narrowed, and soaring peaks closed in on both sides of the road. The ski slopes, still green at this season, stretched like bald streaks down the mountainsides, separated by wide bands of pine trees.

Within a few minutes they had reached the edge of town, where tourist information places and souvenir shops abounded. At the first main intersection, Dexter turned off, and the car began to climb the mountain's slope, past resort signs and condo complexes.

The street grew narrower and steeper, and Savannah had just begun to wonder how anyone got around this town in the winter when Dexter turned yet again, this time into a wide circular driveway. Behind a screen of spruce trees sat an enormous off-white stucco building, its contemporary lines clean and crisp against the mountain's green bulk.

It was large enough to be a whole development, but there was no sign except a discreet house number on a lamppost by the driveway. A single house number, Savannah noted. And the sidewalk led to a pair of enormous carved doors—obviously a single main entrance.

Savannah looked up at the building in stunned silence. What Dexter Caine called a little hideaway in the mountains wasn't anything like the simple condo she'd expected. This was a full-fledged mansion.

CHAPTER SEVEN

Too late, Savannah remembered talking to Robinson—had that been only yesterday?—about the way Dexter lived. The butler had said something about houses, though Savannah had been too distracted by the mention of a manor in County Cork to really listen. But she was sure, now that she thought it over, that he'd said each house had its own staff—and that certainly indicated there was more than one.

When Dexter had said he liked his creature comforts, Savannah had automatically assumed he meant things like cozy wood fires and fuzzy socks and tall cold drinks on a hot afternoon—the kinds of things she considered necessary to comfortable living. Obviously she was way out of her league.

"I have to stop thinking like a peasant," Savannah muttered. She stared up at the angular bulk of the house.

Dexter grinned at her. "A little overpowering, isn't it? In the winter, though, when everything around it is white, it blends in beautifully." He punched a code into a keypad beside the double doors. The lock clicked, and the doors, despite their size and obvious weight, opened at a touch of his fingertips.

Just inside the house, Savannah stopped to stare. She was standing in a huge sun-washed atrium, which pierced the entire house and stretched fifty feet up to the roofline. On the far wall, a series of enormous triangular windows framed a glorious view of the valley and the mountains beyond.

She was unaware of her tiny moan of appreciation till Dexter asked, "Not a bad piece of art, is it? And unlike a painting, it's impossible to get tired of it because it never looks the same two days in a row. Come on in, and we'll have a drink before lunch. Sherry, or would you prefer something else?''

"How about a cup of tea?" Savannah followed him, trying to look at everything at once. In the center of the open space a spiral staircase soared upward, and also led down to another entire level of the house. Through a screen of potted trees, she thought she caught a glimpse of a swimming pool on the lower floor.

Off to one side of the atrium was a dining room, all white and chrome and silvered glass, with a table big enough to seat fourteen. On the other side of the atrium, set at an angle, was a huge, airy, formal living room with a view just as stunning as that from the atrium and a gray granite fireplace where a fire was already burning.

Savannah went to warm her hands; Dexter walked on through to the next room, which was smaller, less formal, and considerably darker. When Savannah followed, she saw why it had been designed that way; an enormous television screen almost filled one wall.

"I see why you're not worried about something to do when you're snowbound," she said mildly. "You've got enough toys here to entertain a nation. Unless the power goes off, of course."

"That's what the books are for."

The light had been so dim she hadn't even seen the wall of shelves at the far end of the room. Her fingertips itched to start pulling volumes down; she had a conviction that a person's choice of reading material said a great deal about him, and she wanted to know what Dexter's books revealed.

He reached for a button under the edge of the round slab of black marble that served as a coffee table. Soft music swelled from hidden speakers, surrounding them.

A few moments later, a gray-haired woman in a black dress and a crisp white apron silently appeared. "Welcome home, sir. Good afternoon, miss."

The housekeeper, Savannah deduced. Well, it was some relief to find that everyone was straight about the facts here.

"Or is it ma'am?" the woman went on. "I hesitate to bring it up, sir, but did you know there's a rumor flying that you've gone and gotten married?"

"There does seem to be some confusion about that," Dexter said absently. "I can't think why."

Savannah's jaw dropped. As if he hadn't caused the gossip himself! And surely he wasn't going to let the rumor stand uncorrected. Not here, among his own people....

He went on smoothly, "My—the lady would like tea, Mrs. Newell."

"Certainly, miss." The housekeeper frowned a little in confusion, and added, for good measure, "Ma'am. Is there any particular variety you prefer?"

Mrs. Newell was obviously a graduate of Robinson's school of how to do things, Savannah thought. "Earl Grey, if you have it. If not, don't go to any trouble—anything will do. And why don't you just call me Savannah?" She glared at Dexter. "It'll make things a lot easier."

The housekeeper looked relieved. "Of course, Miss Savannah. What a pretty name. And you, sir?"

"Bring two cups. We'll have lunch in half an hour."

Mrs. Newell nodded and silently faded from the room.

Savannah wheeled to face him. "I can't believe you didn't tell her!"

"Tell her what?" Dexter had opened a drawer in the bottom of the television cabinet and was flipping through a row of compact discs.

Savannah dug her fists into her hips; if she hadn't, she might have hit him. "That we're not married. What the hell do you think I'm talking about? If I end up in the same bedroom with you again—"

"Oh, if that's all that's bothering you, don't worry about it."

She stared at him in utter amazement while he loaded his choices into the disc player. Then she realized what he meant, and she relaxed a little. "Oh, of course. I'd forgotten about Robinson. Dear old Robbie—when he gets here, he'll straighten everything out." She sat down on one end of the semicircular black leather couch and put her head back. She'd neglected to take off her hat; the brim hit the back of the couch and flipped over, landing on the floor. She didn't bother to retrieve it.

"That's not what I meant," Dexter said calmly. "The house has a double master suite, so there's no problem."

Savannah sat up straight. It wasn't easy; the couch was deep and luxurious, engineered to cradle a body in easy comfort for even the longest movie. "You're not going to tell your own staff? Do you do this sort of thing a lot? Bring home mystery ladies, I mean?"

"Of course not. Couldn't you tell Mrs. Newell didn't have the vaguest idea how to act?"

"I thought that was just because I might turn out to be the wife."

"You're reasoning in circles, Savannah. Robinson packed your jeans, didn't he?"

She blinked in surprise. "I suppose so. I doubt he threw them away, since he went to all the trouble to iron them yesterday when they came back from the laundry. Why?"

"I thought we'd go for a hike after lunch."

"Sure. I could use some exercise. And if there happens to be a handy precipice, I might just push you over."

Dexter grinned. "No, you won't. You're enjoying yourself."

"As kidnappings go, it could be worse," she admitted. "But don't get puffed up about it. I still haven't given up on your biography. In fact, I'm already working it out in my head for when you change your mind."

He patted his breast pocket. "Don't forget I've still got your promise. Which, by the way, has been photocopied and stashed in a safe in Las Vegas, as well as faxed to my bank in Switzerland—just in case you take it into your head to steal into my bedroom some night to get it back."

"That would be unethical."

His eyes lit with mischief. "I just thought I'd mention it, so I'll know if you do steal into my bedroom some night, it isn't that promise you're after."

"In your dreams, Caine."

"Are you certain it's *my* dreams we're talking about? The way you greeted me that first night—"

"I'm not the one who started that," Savannah said firmly.

He looked her over with a slow, sultry smile. "Oh, but my dear, you were. You kissed me as if you hadn't been touched in a year."

Savannah could feel warm color washing over her face, but before she could find an answer, Mrs. Newell returned. This time there was a younger woman with her, wearing a similar black-and- white uniform and carrying a tray set with a stark white china tea set. The china was far from ordinary, however; each piece was triangular.

When they had gone as silently as they had come, Savannah stirred a lump of sugar into her tea and tasted it. It was Earl Grey, of course; she was not surprised. "Come to think of it, I never promised not to write a novel about you."

"Are you attempting to change the subject, Savannah?"

She tried to ignore him. "That's it. I'll do a thinly fictionalized account of your life, and...."

"Nobody'd believe it."

He was probably right, Savannah thought. Fiction still had to be plausible. "Well, then, I guess it'll have to be Cassie's life story after all. As told to Savannah Seabrooke . . . it'll be a bestseller."

"Why were you so interested in Cassie that you tracked down the story about saving the woman's life? You apparently didn't use it. I don't remember that incident being mentioned in anything but the tabloids."

Savannah choked on her tea. "Then you do read them after all? Anyway, I was just interested because it was background on you."

"That's been two years, Savannah. You were interested in me even then?"

"Oh, yes. You're a big subject." She remembered the fleeting feeling she'd had aboard the plane, about how it would take years to get to know him well, and that odd sadness flickered through her again.

"That's flattering."

She smiled a little. "That's my business," she corrected. She leaned forward to refill her cup. "How did you get started, Dexter? Nobody seems to know that."

"Oh, it's a long and boring story."

"It looks as if I'm going to have a week or two to kill," Savannah said dryly. "Oh, and by the way—I've got a couple of articles almost ready to mail. Nothing exciting, I promise. Can I just give them to Robinson?"

The corner of Dexter's mouth turned up just a little. "Oh, please, let me read them first, darling. I'd be honored to be able to take a look at your work."

"That's called censorship, you know."

"No, it's called self-protection. Surely you're not surprised?"

"No, I expected it somehow. So how did you get started?"

"Don't you ever give up?"

"No, especially once I realize that a particular question annoys the person I'm interviewing. And since I now know that you don't want to tell me...."

"It's not that I won't answer, you understand. It's just that talking about myself gives me heartburn, so if you'll wait till after lunch...." He rose and offered a hand to help her up.

"After lunch, I'll be too busy looking for a precipice," she reminded him.

Dexter took a step forward as he tugged her up from the deep couch, and as Savannah came to her feet she found herself almost pressed against him, with their clasped hands held hard against his chest. For a long moment she looked up at him, her breath catching oddly as if her throat was lined with sandpaper. He was watching her lips.

A movement in the doorway caught her eye, and she turned her head quickly.

The housekeeper was waiting. "Luncheon is served, sir."

Dexter didn't move. "Thank you, Mrs. Newell."

He knew she was there, Savannah thought with an odd mixture of relief and annoyance. The relief was because he'd obviously staged that little maneuver on purpose, and so—thank heaven—she didn't have to worry if he'd had any other motives. And the annoyance was because she didn't like being put on display just to make some point to the housekeeper.

And was she also annoyed, just a little, because he *didn't* mean a bit of this byplay?

She bit her lip and pushed the idea away. She was quite sure she didn't want to take a good look at that possibility.

Robinson was bustling around the luncheon table, which was set, Savannah noted, just as the one in Las Vegas had been—with her place at Dexter's right, rather than at the far end. It looked like a romantic gesture, keeping her close to his side, but it was also the place a guest of honor would be seated. It was just another tiny way to keep even his staff guessing, she reflected. Dexter Caine was a champion at that sort of thing.

She unfolded her napkin and smiled at Robinson as he filled her wineglass. He gave her a respectful but brief nod.

He's tightened up again, she thought. I'll have to work on that. Of course, she reminded herself, Robinson was an executive here, with employees looking to him for an example of proper conduct, so he wasn't about to get caught being too friendly with…whatever Savannah was.

She sighed. This whole episode was beginning to make her feel like a nonperson. No doubt, within a month she'd be convinced the entire thing had been nothing more than a dream.

After lunch, Dexter dismissed the hovering staff and showed Savannah up the spiral stairs himself to the master suite, which occupied more than half of the floor. The bedroom he showed her was enormous, light and airy, with French doors opening onto a small balcony with yet another superb view of the valley. The posts of the canopy bed, though traditional in shape and style, were made of glass. The whole thing looked like a delicate ice sculpture draped in drifting lace.

"Well, isn't this cozy?" Savannah said. "Take the bed out and you could play basketball in this room."

"Now there's a thought," Dexter murmured. "And what an original way of suggesting that you'd like to join me next door in *my* room tonight. Savannah, I'm honored. I'm touched. I'm—"

"You're out of your mind."

He smiled. "Half an hour to change your clothes? I'll be waiting."

Savannah closed the door behind him and looked around. She had been only half-kidding about the basketball game. The room was huge, and the colors—icy white and silver, with faint touches of forest green and purple—made it look even larger. Aside from the bed and a couple of sculptured chairs near the French doors, there was no furniture.

She went looking and found a large and luxurious dressing room and an even more sinfully exotic bathroom. The tub was a pink marble whirlpool, big enough for two. Invitingly draped over a rack nearby was a soft velour robe and a couple of bath sheets. On the rim of the tub was a basket full of goodies—lotions and shampoos and bubble bath. She was tempted to try it out, but Dexter had said half an hour. She suspected his patience might not last much longer than that, and she didn't want to find out what he'd do if she was late.

The dressing room was completely lined with closets, and she found her jeans hanging neatly from a trousers hanger. She'd thought Dexter had bought her an awful lot of clothes, but the selection made barely a splash of color in the big cabinets.

She opened them all, and found nothing except what Robinson had packed this morning in Las Vegas. But then, that wasn't surprising; a staff as well trained as Dexter's wouldn't have to be told to sweep all evidence of one woman away before another appeared.

As Dexter had pointed out, however, the housekeeper hadn't quite known how to treat Savannah. Did that mean she wasn't used to him bringing home female guests—or was it just the rumor that had disturbed Mrs. Newell's poise?

Must have been the rumor, Savannah thought. It certainly had thrown everyone else for a loop—including Savannah herself.

It felt good to be wearing her jeans once more, even though she suspected Robinson had not only ironed them but added a bit of starch. She did a couple of deep knee bends to loosen them up, and added a sweater under her dark blue wool jacket. That should be adequate for a walk on a sunny day, she thought. Besides, surely even Dexter hadn't intended her to wear a mink jacket for a hike.

When she came out of the dressing room, the first thing she saw was Dexter, standing on the balcony outside her window. It must open off his room, as well, she concluded. His back was to her, and he was leaning over the edge as if looking down at something far below.

He heard her and turned as she opened the door to join him. A stray breeze caught his hair and tumbled a lock over his forehead, and he smiled—a real smile, she thought, neither teasing nor watchful for a change, but as if he was genuinely glad to see her.

The night before, she had thought him handsome in his tuxedo, under the brilliant casino lights. When they left the hotel, she had thought him extremely good-looking in his dark suit and the tie that so subtly emphasized the red of her dress. Now, he was wearing jeans and a half-zipped denim jacket over a plaid flannel shirt, and she thought he looked even more attractive this way—because suddenly he was real, not a figure from a fantasy anymore. And that made him far more dangerous than ever before.

He held out a hand. "Come here. I want to show you something."

Keep your distance, Savannah, she told herself. It's the only sensible thing to do.

But the sage words were unheeded; she went to him as unavoidably as if the force of gravity had turned suddenly sideways.

He slipped an arm about her waist and drew her close to him against the cool concrete of the balcony. He pointed over the barrier to a narrow ledge four feet below them, where a tiny animal with a distinct stripe down his back crouched on his back legs, looking up with wary anticipation. The ledge was hardly wide enough for him to turn around. Below it was flat stucco wall and the tops of the spruce trees that screened the house.

"A chipmunk," Savannah said. "How sweet! How'd he get up there?"

"Oh, they can climb sheer walls if there's a reason—and he's got plenty of reason." Dexter reached in his pocket and dropped a peanut over the ledge. It landed with a bounce a few inches from the chipmunk, who crept up to sniff it warily and then stuffed it into his cheek before sitting up to beg once more.

Dexter laughed. "Greedy little thing, aren't you? That's six peanuts you've tucked away in two minutes. Leave me some for your buddies up on the mountain, okay?"

The path they took started almost at the back of the house and wound upward at an incredible angle. Within minutes, despite the deliberate pace Dexter set, Savannah was winded and panting.

He paused. "Aren't you used to walking?"

"Of course I am." Savannah dropped onto a log beside the path. "But in case you've never noticed, compared to this little trek, Michigan Avenue is as flat as a pancake."

"I guess that would make a difference," he conceded. He sat down beside her. He wasn't even breathing hard.

"You really love this, don't you?" she accused. "Altitude, thin oxygen, chilly air and all."

Dexter nodded. The path had turned so they could no longer see the house. From their log, only a fragment of the valley was visible, but it was enough to appreciate the lush beauty of the spruces and pines that lined the lower slopes of the mountains. An occasional car horn or the low grind of a truck's gears were the only reminders that they weren't alone in an untouched world.

"And especially the quiet," Dexter said. "Of course, it's not so quiet once ski season starts."

"Where do you go then? The Riviera?"

He smiled a little. "At times I enjoy lying on a beach, of course. There are a couple in Hawaii that I especially like. But—"

"I bet you own them."

"The beaches? No. Well, just little pieces of them."

"I knew it." Savannah pushed herself up from the log. "Where are we headed anyway? All the way to the top?"

"Oh, no. The path climbs another thousand feet or so and then loops around and back down into Winter Park."

"Only another thousand feet straight up? What a relief."

He kept the pace slower after that, and finally the path leveled out and Savannah could actually talk again. "How long are you planning to carry on this charade that we might actually be married?" she asked.

"As long as it takes. Since the tabloids come out only once a week—"

"It wasn't the tabloids I meant, actually. Why haven't you at least told your own people the truth?"

"Honey, I learned a long time ago that the fewer people who share a secret, the less chance there is that someone will let it slip. And though I'm reasonably sure my people are loyal, I don't pay them to be conspirators, and I think it's unlikely they'd be good at it. If they knew the truth, all some smart newspaper person would have to do is make up to one of the maids and mention that you're not quite what you seem, or not quite good enough for me. Don't look horror-stricken, Savannah. You must have made that kind of insinuation yourself, so you know how the game works."

She cleared her throat. "That's beside the point."

"What's the matter? Does it feel different when you're the target? Then the maid, without even thinking, would probably say, 'It's nice of you to be concerned, but don't worry, he hasn't really married her after all,' and the reporter has exactly what he needs. My staff does tend to protect me, you see. Sometimes it backfires."

Savannah frowned. "I suppose you're right, but... You do plan to straighten it all out eventually, don't you?"

"Oh, yes—eventually. Why? Are you worried about your reputation being destroyed?"

She smiled a little. "Some people will no doubt think it's been enhanced instead."

"Modesty forbids me to agree—or even to comment. That's the top of the path and now we start back down. It's a nice little one-mile walk, don't you think?"

"Do you mean it's a mile long or a mile straight up?" Savannah muttered. She found that walking down wasn't a great deal easier than the climb had been; the slope of the uneven ground made the muscles in the back of her legs hurt. Still, she had to admit the sheer beauty of the place was worth the physical discomfort. And if Dexter was an example, climbing that route regularly would take most of the pain out of the effort.

Of course, she reminded herself, she wouldn't have a chance to find out for herself if that was true. It would take longer than a week or two to get her body conditioned, and by then she'd no doubt be home.

And she'd better not forget it.

Robinson was waiting for them with a sheaf of phone messages. "Mitchell called from Australia, sir. Several times."

Dexter took one look at the stack and groaned.

Savannah said sweetly, "Since I'm sure you don't want me hanging around for this little business conference, sweetheart, I think I'll go check out the whirlpool you so thoughtfully provided in my bathroom."

"It's unkind of you to point out that you'll be luxuriating while I work," Dexter called after her.

Savannah leaned over the railing at the top of the spiral stairs. "But, darling, I did tell you not to fire poor Peter. Just think, if he were here—"

Dexter set a foot on the lowest step. "He could take care of all this, and I could join you in the whirlpool."

Savannah swallowed hard at the sensations that particular vision created.

Dexter laughed. "No, I haven't hired him back. But you're giving me a whole lot to think about, my dear."

Savannah was very careful to lock the bathroom door. But she thoroughly enjoyed her long soak, followed by a nap, and by dinnertime her equilibrium was restored.

Beef Wellington didn't hurt her mood, either, and the sliver of raspberry cheesecake that followed was the perfect finishing touch. "In fact," she confided to Dexter as they rose from the table, "if you've got a cappuccino machine hidden somewhere around here, I'd consider myself in heaven."

"I haven't the vaguest idea," he said, and led her into the television room once more. He was still selecting music and asking about her preferences when Robinson appeared with two cups of cappuccino.

I could get used to all this, Savannah thought. It was almost like magic; cars and even airplanes simply materialized when they were needed, and then vanished till the next time. Clean clothing appeared in her closet without her ever seeing the hands that put it there. She'd murmured something about cappuccino, and the next thing she knew, there it was in front of her, frothy and picture perfect.

"That will be all for tonight, Robinson," Dexter said. After the butler was gone, he came to sit beside Savannah on the deep leather couch and slipped an arm around her shoulders. "That sounded like a sigh of satisfaction."

She tensed a little. "I like my cappuccino, that's all."

He kissed her lightly, tracing the line of her lips with the tip of his tongue. "It tastes good, true. But you taste better."

It seemed impossible that such a soft and gentle caress could have the power to set off earthquakes inside her. "Why did you do that?" Savannah whispered. "There's no one to impress."

For a moment, as he kissed the corner of her mouth, she thought he wasn't going to answer. But finally he murmured, "I never said I didn't enjoy playing with fire now and then, Savannah."

Suddenly, firmly, his lips took hers. He was neither demanding nor begging, simply expecting that she would respond. And she did exactly that; unable to deny the effect he had on her, she slid her fingers up through his hair and pulled him closer.

He nibbled her ear and whispered, "All afternoon I've been thinking of you in that whirlpool. Which, of course, is exactly what you wanted me to think. You did that on purpose, didn't you?"

She pulled back a little—as far as she could, for he was holding her very close indeed—and shook her head. "I didn't."

"Then why did you say it?" He lifted her chin so she had to look at him. "Because you like to play with fire, too, Savannah. If you didn't, you would never have walked into Peter's office, or gotten on board the plane at O'Hare."

Her gaze fell. She suspected he was right about that.

"So where do we go from here?" His fingertips feathered down her throat and paused over the hollow at the base, where her pulse fluttered wildly. "I don't see any reason we shouldn't light a few matches. Do you?"

"You mean—have an affair," she said flatly.

"For someone who has a gift for words, my dear, that's such an insipid way of putting it. Why not just say we'll enjoy each other and see what happens?"

His lips followed the path his fingertips had traced, and she wouldn't have been surprised to feel blisters forming in his wake. Hunger rose in her. She wanted to taste him again. She wanted....

That was when Savannah really began to wonder about her sanity.

She shook her head abruptly and slid away from him, almost to the end of the leather couch. She sat there very straight, not able to move farther and not daring to look at him, though she knew he was watching her. She could feel his gaze moving over her; it was as real a sensation as if he had been stroking her bare skin.

"When you change your mind," he said huskily, "let me know."

The words seemed to break the spell. Savannah didn't look at him as she bolted up the spiral stairs to the nominal security of her own bedroom.

Now that the sunlight was gone, the room felt cold. It wasn't a physical chill; the air was warm enough. This was a frigidity born of loneliness, as if despite its beauty this room had never been used at all, and thus had never had a chance to assume a personality.

As if, Savannah thought, it was still waiting for the woman who would make it live.

And you think you might be that woman? she jeered at herself.

She was truly a fool if she allowed herself to think that way for even a moment. Playing with fire—that was all Dexter was doing. Taking chances was his nature after all, just as it was hers; he'd been right about that much. He'd seen the similarities, but he hadn't recognized the differences.

Dexter would make sure he wasn't burned—but what about Savannah?

His caution was innate; hers didn't come naturally. He bet on himself and relied on his skills to improve the odds. She did things all or nothing, with no middle ground and sometimes without much consideration of the outcome. If Dexter thought he was playing with fire, then Savannah was toying with a nuclear explosion.

And what if it was already too late to stop?

CHAPTER EIGHT

SAVANNAH didn't sleep well. Though the canopy bed was firm and comfortable, the glass-pillared bedposts, combined with her earlier sense that the room was frigid and lonely, made her feel cold, and even the extra blankets she found in the dressing-room closets couldn't comfort her. Only when light began to creep through the sheer curtains—later and much dimmer than it had been in Las Vegas because of the overshadowing mountains—did she drift off completely and find herself untroubled by dreams.

It was very late indeed when she woke, but the moment she pushed the curtains back she saw why she had slept so long. Fog blanketed the whole valley, filling every rift between the mountains with a deep, thick mist.

From her bedroom windows, despite their location high on the slope, Savannah could barely see over the mist. From the atrium on the main level, the view had vanished altogether, as if the house had been wrapped in tissue paper.

From the dining room, she heard Dexter's voice, full of exasperation. "Because I'm fogged in, that's why. It would take hours just to drive to Denver."

There was no answer, so Savannah deduced he must be on the phone.

"What do you think I pay you for anyway?" he went on impatiently. "If there's a reason you can't handle this yourself, perhaps we'd better reconsider the terms of your employment contract." There was a pause, and then he added, "If it was only *my* money you were playing with, I wouldn't be so upset!"

Savannah gave a soundless whistle and dawdled on the atrium balcony till she heard the distinctive bang of a telephone receiver. She even debated retreating to her room and ringing for Robinson rather than venture into the dining room.

On the other hand, she might as well brave the bear in his den; she'd have to face him sometime. And it might be interesting to see the unflappable Dexter Caine in a royal temper. From what she'd read, even his employees found it a rare sight indeed. Fury, one of them had said once, usually just made him more icily polite—and correspondingly even more dangerous.

He only half rose from his chair as Savannah came in, and his reply to her good-morning was no more than a grunt. She poured herself a cup of coffee at the sideboard and eyed him warily.

He was dressed casually this morning, in a dark blue sweater with multicolored diamonds knitted into the front, and corduroy trousers. Newspapers were strewn over the table. His plate had been pushed aside with half a waffle still uneaten, and the telephone and a sheaf of paper that looked like a contract had taken its place. Now he refolded the pages, tossed them atop the disorganized mess in his open briefcase, and rubbed the bridge of his nose. "Sit down."

"I can't," Savannah pointed out. "Your briefcase is occupying my chair, and I don't dare touch it for fear you'll accuse me of espionage on top of all my other supposed infractions." She eyed the papers. Reading upside down was a talent she'd tried to cultivate, with little success. But she'd swear that contract said something about a foundation, and an institute, and inner-city housing....

"Sorry." He stood up to move the briefcase and hold her chair. "Though you couldn't use what you found out anyway, you know. You promised."

"Actually, I think you're wrong about that."
Savannah stirred her coffee. "A promise given under
duress isn't really binding. Besides, I only promised not
to use what you told me—I didn't say a thing about what
I might see lying around. Though I could be wrong. Since
I don't even have a copy of that piece of paper I signed,
I can't review it to be sure."

His eyes were bright. "I suppose you want me to go
get it so you can search for loopholes?"

"Only if you'll leave me alone with your briefcase in
the meantime." Savannah waved a hand toward the huge
windows. "Nice view."

"Just like floating in the clouds."

"Or being stuck in the middle of a marshmallow. And
I thought snow would be the biggest problem up here."

"Usually the fog hangs around the tops of the mountains. It keeps the plane grounded, but at least it's safe
to drive. This is an unusually heavy one." Dexter picked
up a newspaper from the mess at his elbow and thrust
it at her. "Take a look at the gossip column."

"You mean the serious media picked this up, too? I
thought they'd wait till the middle of the week when the
first tabloids come out." Savannah sipped her coffee and
studied the column he'd pointed out. The item was tiny,
just a couple of inches of type with a small photograph
of the two of them at dinner in Las Vegas, and a headline
that said "Call Her Mrs.?".

"Not a bad picture," she conceded.

Dexter's eyebrows soared. "It doesn't even really look
like you."

"That's what I mean. If it did, things would be a good
deal worse." Savannah refolded the paper so only the
gossip column showed and read the story aloud.
"'Billionaire Dexter Caine took Las Vegas by surprise
over the weekend when he seemed to announce that the
mystery lady having dinner with him is his wife. But star-
watchers say they've never seen her before, and noted

that neither Caine nor the mystery lady was wearing a ring...."' She set the paper aside and shook her head sadly. "I ought to have expected that someone as inexperienced as you when it comes to matrimony would overlook something as obvious as a ring."

"Damn. Who'd have thought they'd pick up on a petty detail like that?"

"Dexter darling, where the media are concerned, there are no petty details. Now that you've given them a reason to be interested, they'll spare no effort to find out what you're up to. I tried to tell you that, but you wouldn't listen. The tabloids have no doubt blown those pictures up to poster size and gone over them with a magnifying glass. If one of us happens to need a dental filling, they'll probably know it before we do."

"How do you know so much about how the tabloids operate? Have you done a story on them?"

Savannah's breath caught for just a moment. "Something like that."

But Dexter wasn't listening; he'd picked up the newspaper again. "I suppose now we'll have to come up with a ring. Or better yet, two—engagement and wedding."

"Don't you think a knee-jerk reaction like that would look suspicious? Why don't you just let it slip that you're very disappointed because I refuse to wear a ring?"

"Any woman that I'd—"

"Please," Savannah interrupted. "Spare me. I've only had half a cup of coffee, so I'm simply not yet up to contemplating what the women you'd be interested in would do in this situation. Hold you up for a ten-carat rock probably."

He regarded her with a thoughtful little wrinkle between his brows. "Don't you like rings, Savannah?"

"That is beside the point. Men refuse to wear wedding rings all the time and nobody gets upset. Why should it be a problem if a woman doesn't want to wear one?"

"What kind of ring do you like best?"

She sighed. "You're just like wallpaper paste, you know that, Caine? You're all over the subject and impossible to get rid of. Where's Robinson, by the way? If I'm going to have to argue about this, I'd like to have a little food first."

As if in answer, the butler came in with two plates; each held a thick, fresh, hot, whole-grain waffle garnished with chunks of fruit. "If you'd prefer something else, Miss Savannah...." he began.

"No, this looks perfectly fine to me." She stabbed a chunk of honeydew melon and ate it while Robinson rearranged Dexter's place, set the fresh plate in front of him, and removed the used one. "You're thoroughly spoiled, you know," she said.

"Undoubtedly." Dexter didn't move to pick up his fork. "What kind of ring, Savannah?"

She paused with a bite of pineapple halfway to her mouth and debated. This was a genuinely bad idea; she wasn't quite sure why, but she was convinced of it. Apparently, however, nothing was going to change Dexter's mind. So what sort of ring could she demand that would be difficult—or, if she was lucky, even impossible—to get? Something outlandish, something no jeweler in his right mind would create....

"An opal, I think," she said. "With diamonds and emeralds—oh, and a cluster of pearls—surrounding it."

The corner of Dexter's mouth quivered a little, as if he knew exactly what was in her mind. "Robinson, somewhere in the storage loft is a jewelry box. It's about twelve inches square, and the top is inlaid wood. Bring it to me, please."

She sighed. "You don't really have an opal ring tucked away somewhere, do you?"

"I don't know. We'll find out. If not, maybe we'll find something else you could stand to wear." He started to eat. "Have you lost your appetite, dear? We can't exactly go downtown and shop, you know. If you're right about the tabloids' attention to detail, they'll probably have the jewelry stores staked out." He looked at her thoughtfully. "Didn't you start to tell me how you know so much about how those people think?"

Savannah shrugged. "I read up on their methods once. Just checking out the competition. Now and then they have a good idea on how to investigate."

Dexter grinned. "So that's where you learned to bluff your way past personal assistants, hmm? Ah, thank you, Robinson."

The wooden box the butler presented looked as if it had been polished within the past five minutes. The inlaid pattern on the lid formed a dainty, intricate mosaic of lilies and daisies, made of a dozen types of wood that Savannah couldn't identify.

It was full of costume jewelry from two generations ago—rhinestone bracelets, their brilliance dimmed by age and accumulated dust, and intricate, bright-colored crystals set into scarf clips and hair ornaments. There was a garish gold leopard pin with malevolent bright green eyes. And there were necklaces in a half-dozen different colors and styles.

Savannah plucked out a circular pin set with rather dingy rhinestones and stuck it on the ring finger of her left hand. "How's this?"

Dexter hardly spared it a glance. "Doesn't fit very well."

"Well, you can't have everything." She tossed the pin back and picked up an enormous earring covered with a cluster of dark red stones. She clipped it on her earlobe. "What fun! I'd have given my right arm for this assortment when I was a child and still played dress-up at every opportunity."

A half smile tugged at Dexter's lips. "Well...yes, I can understand that." He dug into a corner and picked up a ring. "An opal, I believe." He held it out to her. "Unless you'd rather have something different after all.

There's also a cameo, I see, or...whatever this is." He picked up a gold ring set with a strange orange-colored stone and frowned at it.

Reluctantly, Savannah took the opal ring. She had no doubt that it was real; though the stone was every bit as large and attention-getting as the costume jewelry, the opal seemed to glow in the misty daylight. The deep greens and blues and the smaller markings of pink and red and yellow made the stone look like a photo of the world taken from space—except that it was oval instead of round. The opal was set in gold and surrounded by small clear stones.

"No pearls in the setting, or emeralds," Dexter said, "but there are enough diamonds to make up for it, I believe."

Savannah stared at the row of diamonds. They were dull, in need of a good cleaning, but there was no denying what they were. Then she looked more closely at the tangled mass in the box, and gulped. What she had thought must be rhinestones—because there were so awfully many of them—were also dusty diamonds.

She pulled off the earring to study it. No costume jewel had ever shown the fire that gleamed deep inside the red stones. They were rubies, of a size Savannah had never even dreamed of. Her fingers trembled, and she dropped the earring back into the box as if it had actually burned her.

"Something wrong?" Dexter asked.

"That stuff's real!"

"Of course it is. My grandmother would have been very upset if people thought anything else."

His grandmother? Then there had been family money backing him—and from the look of things, no shortage of it, since he hadn't sold these jewels long ago to fund his start in business. Savannah could picture an aristocratic old lady, drenched in valuable gems, with Dexter at her knee learning how to deal with money, and position, and servants....

Dexter was digging through the box as he spoke. "Here—try this one along with the opal." He held out a plain, heavy gold ring rimmed with diamonds.

A mock wedding band, Savannah thought, and shook her head. "Dexter, I can't explain why I feel as I do, but this is a really bad idea."

He picked up her hand and slipped the diamond band on her finger, then added the opal ring as a guard. "I think you've simply got a case of nerves. The rings look wonderful."

"What about one for you? If I've got to do this—"

"You said it yourself, darling. A lot of men don't wear wedding rings." He rose. "I have to go now. See you at lunch. You might ask Robinson to clean those stones— they'd look better if they sparkled."

Savannah called after him, "How about sending them to a jeweler for a professional job? That way, the word will get out about the heirlooms you're giving me, and it'll help explain why the rings haven't appeared till now. Since we had to come back here to get them...."

And if she was lucky, a professional would take days to clean the rings and check the settings, and she might not have to wear them at all. She felt foolish about her hesitation, though. The rings were beautiful, and any woman in her right mind would grab the chance to wear them. Why did she feel so strongly about putting them on?

Dexter came back into the dining room and leaned over her chair. "See? When you let yourself go, Savannah, you have some really good ideas. We'll take them downtown ourselves after lunch, and wait while they're cleaned. Now that you've finally got your rings, you won't want to be without them long, I'm sure." His lips brushed her cheek as softly as a dream, and he was gone.

Savannah stared down at her hand. Even an amateur could tell this was a first-rate jewel. No amount of dust could hide the beauty of the opal or the soft gleam of gold in the diamond-rimmed band. Dexter's grandmother's taste in settings might have been a bit garish by modern standards, but she'd certainly known quality stones when she saw them.

Savannah wondered how the woman would feel about her jewelry being used to pull a prank on the world. Not pleased, she'd bet. Hadn't Dexter said something about his grandmother—like Savannah's own mother—being an expert at producing guilt?

The two rings fit together better than she would have expected, though they were a little loose on her finger. She'd have to be very careful when she wore them— which would be only when it was absolutely necessary, she decided. It would be too easy to lose them.

It would also be too easy, she admitted, to get used to the weight of them, and forget that these—like the magnificent necklace she'd worn in Las Vegas—were only loaned to her for a brief time. No doubt her hesitation to put them on at all had sprung from the last remaining vestige of her common sense.

She turned her hand and watched as the diamonds caught weakly at the light. How beautiful they'd be when they were clean and sparkling.

How beautiful this would all be, if it were only real.

She bit her lip hard. The pain helped to mask the ache in her heart, but there was no longer any way to mask the truth.

In the space of a few days, in this surreal atmosphere, as she pretended to be the woman Dexter Caine loved, Savannah had come to wish she was that woman. Last night she had wondered if it might be too late to stop playing with danger. Today she knew her instinct had been right—it was far, far too late.

Dexter Caine had taken over her life; that was a temporary phenomenon, and sooner or later it would end. But Savannah had allowed him to creep into her heart. She had fallen in love with him—and that complication, she knew, would never go away.

They didn't go to the jewelry store together, for lunchtime brought not Dexter but a note, delivered by Robinson.

Savannah was in the living room waiting for Dexter, reading a magazine and luxuriating in the beauty and warmth of a fire, when the butler brought in an envelope. Her throat tightened in fear, and even after she read the note she didn't feel much better. Dexter's business crisis had gotten worse since breakfast, and it required his personal attention, so he was taking advantage of a momentary break in the weather to fly to....

"He's gone to Newark?" she asked uncertainly, looking up at Robinson in dismay. "As in New Jersey? In that fog?"

"Yes, miss. He said to tell you there simply wasn't time to take you. The plane had to go right then or it might not have gotten off the ground at all. Flying in these mountains is tricky enough without fog interfering."

"I know—I'm worried about him." She added hastily, "And the crew, of course."

And I miss him already, she thought. How am I going to stand it when this week or two is over, and I never see him again? A bleak chill settled in her chest.

She added firmly, "But I certainly don't feel left out. After all, he didn't even take you this time."

"It's not a terribly exciting destination anyway, miss."

"No manor houses?"

Robinson allowed himself a tiny smile. "Not in Newark. Mr. Caine doesn't even keep a permanently reserved hotel suite there, I'm afraid."

"I expect," Savannah mused, "that he's much more interested in other kinds of housing there. In fact, this really isn't a business trip at all, is it?"

Robinson looked shocked. "I beg your pardon, miss—"

"I mean," she went on smoothly, "Mr. Caine's foundation isn't what you'd call a money-*making* business. Right?"

The butler unbent a little. "That's quite true. But the institute has done a great deal of good in the inner city, miss."

Savannah wished he'd at least let the name slip. She was dead sure it wasn't listed under Caine; if Dexter had put his name on a foundation, she'd have found it long ago. She wondered how he'd have managed to keep her in the dark if the fog hadn't provided a handy excuse to leave her at home....

The word caught at her throat. How easy it would be to look at this house as *home*... and how dangerous to her peace of mind. "When will he be back?" She hoped the question didn't sound forlorn.

"By Wednesday afternoon, I expect. Certainly in time for the party."

Savannah blinked and dropped her magazine. "What party?"

Robinson didn't seem surprised at her reaction. "Mr. Caine gave orders for a small cocktail party on Wednesday evening for a few of the neighbors. Do you have any suggestions or requests?"

Cancel it, Savannah wanted to say. What was Dexter up to now anyway? If there was the slightest chance he wasn't going to be back in time.... "Not a thing, Robinson. I'm sure you'll handle it beautifully."

"Yes, Miss Savannah. If you think of anything you'd like concerning the menu or entertainment...."

"I'll certainly let you know," she murmured.

She picked at her lunch, and afterward retreated to her room to finish working on her articles and get them ready to mail to the magazines that had commissioned the work. If she was lucky, a check from one or the other of them might be waiting for her when she finally got home. It would certainly make it easier to face her landlord if she could actually pay her rent.

And concentrating on her work helped—though only minimally—to keep her mind off Dexter, too.

It was midafternoon when she went looking for Robinson to find out how to mail her packages; despite what Dexter had said about wanting to censor her articles to be certain they had nothing to do with him, surely he wouldn't expect her to wait till he got back, would he?

The house was quiet, with none of the staff in evidence. Every surface gleamed; not so much as a fingerprint marred the shining chrome handrail of the spiral staircase. The fire in the living room had been allowed to die down to embers. The rooms were silent.

For a while she actually thought she might be alone. She walked through the dining room and the butler's pantry and still found no Robinson, though the soft gleam of silver and china behind glass doors testified to his attention to detail.

She pushed open a swinging door to a huge stainless-steel kitchen, and heard a young man say, "Do you suppose he's really married her?" Savannah thought she recognized the voice; the young man had lit the fire for her this morning.

"It's not proper for you to speculate," Mrs. Newell said repressively.

"Doesn't seem likely, though." This voice was also masculine, but faintly accented. "It appears that nobody in any of the houses has caught a glimpse of her before this weekend, or even suspected she existed. And yet suddenly we're supposed to believe he's married her?"

Savannah pushed the door a little wider. The chef was standing at a large work island with his back almost against the door. Mrs. Newell was sitting at the table with a cup of tea in front of her. A woman was chopping vegetables at one of the sinks; the young man was cleaning up the discarded leaves and tops.

The chef went on, "I think he's just entertaining himself. And heaven knows she'd be entertaining. She—"

Savannah knew the instant the woman at the sink saw her, for a soft shushing noise cut across the chef's voice. Mrs. Newell looked up in horror. The chef stopped talking in midword and swung around to face Savannah. He was moving so fast that a glob of whipped cream spun off the spatula he was holding and hit her squarely across the upper lip.

Savannah was glad it didn't catch her in the eyes; she'd have hated to miss the expression on the chef's face. Stunned disbelief at the accident gave way to embarrassment and then to fear as he realized that she must have overheard what he'd been saying. She could see him replaying his comments in his mind and wondering whether she had the power to fire him.

Everyone in the kitchen seemed frozen. Savannah stood perfectly still for several seconds, then wiped the lump of whipped cream off her lip with her index finger and popped it in her mouth. "Not bad," she said. "Perhaps it needs to be a little sweeter, depending on what you're doing with it."

The chef's Adam's apple bobbed. "I'm making a trifle, Miss Savannah. Ma'am."

"'Miss Savannah' will do just fine. You don't need to be scared of me, you know. I'm certainly not going to fire you, because I'd have to explain to Mr. Caine when he gets home why he's having take-out Chinese for dinner." She dipped another finger into the whipped-cream bowl, smiled up at the chef, and drew a white mustache across his upper lip. "There. We're even. And if you really want to get in my good graces, I'd love a big juicy bratwurst with sauerkraut on the side for dinner. Does anyone know where I'll find Robinson?"

Mrs. Newell seemed to come back to life. "In his apartment, Miss Savannah. I'll call him."

"Don't disturb him. Whenever he reappears, just tell him I've got a question."

The silence in the kitchen was complete, but the moment the door shut behind Savannah she heard an indistinct murmur of voices, and then an accented one, which rose above the others. "Now that," the chef said, "is a lady. If he hasn't married her, I certainly hope he plans to."

Savannah smiled a little, but her eyes stung. "Not likely," she whispered.

Dexter might find her entertaining, as even the chef seemed to know. He might enjoy the idea of playing with fire by having an affair with her. But he'd said himself—indirectly, perhaps, but on more than one occasion—that Savannah wasn't the sort of person he was looking for when it came to more than a temporary arrangement.

"Any woman I'd be interested in," he'd said before their shopping spree, "wouldn't consider buying her clothes at a discount store." He'd have said almost the same thing this morning about jewelry if she hadn't stopped him. And no doubt, any woman he'd be interested in wouldn't have a craving for bratwurst and sauerkraut, or get friendly with the butler, or trade whipped-cream mustaches with the chef.

In fact, Savannah couldn't imagine Dexter doing anything of the sort. She tried to picture him swapping off-color stories with his jet pilots, or inviting Robinson to take a seat in the main cabin, or inquiring solicitously about Mrs. Newell's arthritis—but she couldn't begin to do it. Setting up a foundation or making sure a little girl got the therapy she needed were different things altogether.

He wasn't cold; he wasn't uncaring. He simply didn't look at things the same way Savannah did.

And if she was smart, Savannah told herself, she'd remember that they really had nothing in common.

The house felt incredibly empty without him, and soon after dinner Savannah went to her bedroom once more. With her papers scattered around and her computer humming softly, the room was beginning to feel more comfortable. She toyed with several new ideas, but she knew she couldn't settle down to serious work. Now that the two finished stories were on their way to Chicago, only one file drew her attention. Ultimately she surrendered and pulled her list of questions for Dexter up on the screen.

He had answered very few of them. He still hadn't told her how he got his start in business, or which had been the most interesting deal of his life. Or why he had a house in Ireland. Or what challenges he intended to take up next. Or what kept him interested in striving, with so much money already in the bank. Or what had been so special about his grandmother....

She looked down at the rings on her left hand. She had spent an hour that afternoon cleaning them with gentle soap and a soft brush, and now the stones rewarded her with starbursts of dazzling light and fire. She ought to take them off, she knew. She was alone, and there was no reason to wear them right now.

And for her own sake, for her own sanity, she shouldn't let herself dream about wearing them always. Or, even more importantly, dream about having Dexter Caine forever.

With the clarity of hindsight, she could see that even from the very beginning she hadn't merely been attracted to him. She had wanted desperately to know him.

That was why she had stayed, not because of the threats he'd made. And once she had begun to know him and realized that the truth of all her research did not begin to touch the real man he was—well, then she'd begun to want him.

Her jitters on the evening in Las Vegas when they had launched this incredible masquerade had not been fear of the consequences he'd threatened if she didn't live up to his expectations. Oh, no—the truth was that she had wanted him to be impressed with her, as she already was with him. She had been afraid she might disappoint him—and she had already known deep in her heart that she wanted never to do that.

And Dexter? His goals were different; he'd said so himself. He wanted them to enjoy each other, that was all. Have fun together. Play with fire....

Robinson tapped at her door. "Miss Savannah? Mr. Caine is calling."

She grabbed for the phone, telling herself even as she did so that she shouldn't let him realize she felt any eagerness to talk to him.

"Hi." His voice had a rough edge, as if he was tired. "Miss me, Savannah?"

"Of course not." She sounded a bit husky herself. "This is the best resort I've ever stayed in. Who needs company?"

"Robinson tells me you've been mailing things."

"Absolutely." She let a note of surprise creep into her voice. "Didn't you expect me to as soon as your back was turned? I was disappointed, actually—Robinson didn't even bother to read my articles. You left in such a hurry you forgot to tell him to, didn't you?"

"And you were betting on that, no doubt?"

"Of course not," Savannah said cheerfully. "I'd spent hours translating everything into code. That's why I was so disappointed—all that effort wasted. But don't worry. I kept copies for you."

"Which version do I get to read? Coded or regular?"

"Whichever you'd prefer. I'm surprised you took such a chance on the weather, you know. What's so important about Newark? I thought you said you could do all your business by phone and fax."

"This is a personnel problem. It's going to require a little sorting out, but I'll be back as soon as I can."

He didn't offer details; Savannah would have been amazed if he had. "You'd better be back by Wednesday. You're not saddling me with a party and not showing up."

"Robinson told you about that, hmm? What innovations have you added?"

"None. Robinson seems eminently qualified, and it's not my place."

"But it is—you're the hostess."

I wish I truly was, she thought. "Why a party anyway?"

"To introduce you to the neighbors. I'm sure at least some of them have tabloid reporters camped on their doorsteps asking questions, and this will give them something to talk about. Just think, Savannah, it'll make everyone happy. The neighbors, the tabloids, us...."

"You're not making this any easier," Savannah warned.

"I believe in enjoying things while I can. It's not a bad philosophy, you know."

The words stuck in her mind, and after she put down the phone she was still thinking about what he'd said. *I believe in enjoying things while I can.*

And how did that fit with Savannah's way of life?

She added one last question to her list, and looked at it for a long time. Then she slowly began to erase each entry one by one. The questions didn't matter anymore; the only thing she knew—or needed to know—was how important he was to her. She wiped out the entire list, except for that last and most important question. Then she turned off the computer and went to bed.

But the one question that remained was a nagging whisper even in her dreams, as indelibly imprinted on her mind as it was in the mechanical memory of her computer.

Do you think you could ever love me as much as I love you?

CHAPTER NINE

THE house was still as comfortable, the views as spectacular, the living as luxurious—but with Dexter gone, all the life had gone out of the place. By Wednesday, Savannah found herself wandering from room to room, almost driving herself crazy as she tried to occupy her mind and keep from thinking about him.

But the house was full of his presence, and everywhere she turned she saw a reminder of him. When she sat down on the black leather couch in the television room, every cell in her body remembered the way he had held her, and how she had responded to his touch. And she couldn't help wondering what would have happened if her answer had been a different one that night when he had asked her to make love with him.

The odd thing was that Savannah knew as surely as if from firsthand experience what sort of lover he would be. He'd be tender and considerate. He'd be supremely confident, without being demanding or impatient. They'd have all the time in the world to explore the wonders he would show her....

Whoa! she told herself rudely. She was beginning to act and think as if making love with him was inevitable, as if she had no choice left in the matter. And that change in her attitude was dangerous. If she slept with him, she might have a week or two of enjoyment, but she would have to pay for the pleasure with years of memories— and some of them would be less than comfortable. Having an affair with Dexter Caine would only make her life more difficult down the road, and she'd better not forget that fact.

He had told her once that if she dared to talk about the time they spent together he would say she was a former lover who was unhappy at being set aside. Perhaps that was why he had suggested they have an affair—because then, if she ever mentioned their idyll, he could defend himself with simple truth.

And he would be telling the truth, she admitted. If she became his lover, she would be very unhappy indeed when the end came. Not unhappy enough to talk about it publicly, of course. She wasn't the kind to share her private griefs with the world—especially a world that would actually pay for the voyeuristic details. But Dexter couldn't know that.

Not that self-protection was his only motive; Savannah was convinced that if he hadn't expected to enjoy himself with her, he would never have suggested an affair. But nothing said he couldn't have more than one reason for his actions. And though she didn't want to think that he could be so calculating, Savannah knew from her own experience that he could indeed be just that devious. The announcement of their supposed marriage was the most obvious example; the message had been clear, and yet he hadn't really said anything definite at all and so could deny it at any time.

No, the only smart thing for Savannah to do was keep her emotional distance and not allow herself to be thrown off balance by his exhilarating personality. This whole crazy episode would be over soon, and then she could start to get her life back on track.

Of course she was having trouble right now putting him out of her mind, she told herself comfortingly. After all, she was living in his house, surrounded by his aura even though he was half a continent away, and she was far too sensitive to simply ignore it.

But things would be different once she was back in Chicago. There she'd have her friends, her business contacts, her work. She'd be very busy, and with no time

to daydream about Dexter Caine, she'd soon have her
balance back. If she was wise enough not to add to her
long-term pain for the sake of a week or two of pleasure,
she'd soon get over him.

But right now, with nothing to fill the long hours but
thoughts of him....

The staff was little help. They were occupied with party
plans and had no time for entertaining Savannah even
if her pride had allowed her to confess that she was bored
stiff.

She tried to help, but Dexter's employees were so terribly efficient there was nothing for her to do. When she
offered to pitch in and clean, Mrs. Newell looked faintly
horrified. And it took only a few minutes of observing
the delicate, elaborate hors d'oeuvres the chef was pre-
paring by the hundreds to know that her efforts in that
direction would not be particularly helpful.

Savannah thought wistfully of bundling up and going
for a long walk. Maybe she could look around the stores
downtown—if she was careful not to talk to anyone. But
she half expected Dexter had left instructions not to let
her out of the house alone. Not only did she shiver away
from the idea of someone trailing after her like a bodyguard—or worse, a nanny—but she didn't think
Robinson could spare anyone with the party just hours
away.

In any case, she admitted, if she wasn't allowed the
freedom of wandering off by herself, she'd rather not
find out for certain. It would be humiliating to be refused permission to go out; she'd rather keep up the pre-
tense that she was an honored guest.

Savannah, she warned, you're deluding yourself. And
it's getting to a dangerous level.

But the talking-to didn't help much, she realized when
she chose her dress for the party and found herself day-
dreaming over the look she hoped would be in Dexter's
eyes when she came down the stairs wearing it. Surely

he couldn't look at her in that sleek little black crepe number with its plunging neckline and slit skirt and almost nonexistent back and be unimpressed....

On the other hand, she reminded herself firmly, since he'd seen the dress when she'd modeled it at the boutique, there was no reason for him to be impressed when he saw it again.

Finally, in desperate need of a distraction, she curled up by the fire in the living room and called her mother. Connie Seabrooke told her that her landlord had phoned the day before to leave a message for Savannah.

"I'll have to find the slip of paper," Connie said. "I wrote it all down, and it's here somewhere. I wasn't expecting to hear from you till the weekend, so I put it up where it wouldn't get lost in the meantime.... Oh, here it is. Jack's been checking your answering machine, of course. Mostly it's just calls from friends wondering how you've dropped so completely out of sight, but—"

"Terrific," Savannah muttered. She was going to have to come up with the world's greatest cover story in order to explain a couple of weeks' absence. Her mother might believe the bit about a temporary job, but her friends wouldn't—especially when she came back even more broke than she'd been before. And they wouldn't believe she'd gone on vacation, either, because she'd left so abruptly, and would return with no souvenirs and not even a hint of a tan....

On the other hand, if the photos the tabloids used were better shots of her than the first one had been, trying to squeak by with a cover story would only make things worse. Then she'd *really* have some fancy explaining to do.

"But there was one message he thought was important," Connie went on. "Brian from *Today's Woman* magazine has been trying to get hold of you."

Savannah was startled. It would be just her luck if Brian had a change of heart on publishing the story about

Dexter, now that she couldn't go ahead with it. Even though the article predated her promise, she wouldn't care to try to convince Dexter that it wasn't included in their little agreement.

But that wasn't likely, surely. Brian must have something else in mind. Perhaps he had another assignment to give her, or he just wanted to know when she could get that ghastly piece on lead poisoning to him.

"So how's the new job going, dear?" Connie asked.

"It won't last much longer." Savannah wondered even as she said it whether the note of warning in her voice was intended for her mother or for herself. "I'll be home in a week or two."

"Well, it's too bad it won't last. It must be a lovely position if you're free to call me at this hour of a weekday."

That was a detail Savannah hadn't considered having to explain. "Since I don't know where I might be next Sunday, I thought I'd better take advantage of the opportunity."

"I hope you're able to enjoy all this travel," Connie said. "It sounds so exciting. When you get home I'll come up to the city, so we can have lunch and you can tell me all about what you've seen."

"Of course," Savannah said. Her voice sounded hollow, but her mother didn't seem to notice.

Savannah debated whether to call Brian, but she finally decided she'd better; he'd been too steady a source of assignments and income to ignore.

"Savannah?" he said. "Just a minute." He cupped his hand over the mouthpiece, but not securely enough; she could hear him shooing people out of his office. "Where the heck are you?" he went on. "I was beginning to suspect you'd disappeared on purpose."

Savannah's heart stuck in her throat. Had he seen the gossip columns—and the photographs? But even if he had, surely he wouldn't have connected that slightly blurry young woman with her. There must be a hundred people who looked vaguely like that picture.

"I owe you an apology," he went on.

"Oh?" Savannah said cautiously.

"Obviously you knew what you were talking about when it comes to Dexter Caine and Cassie King. I should have trusted your judgment, Savannah. As it stands now—"

She panicked. "Look, Brian, you can't use the story after all."

"Of course not. There's a whole new dimension to it now that Caine's come out into the open a little more. If you can find out who this woman is, and whether he's actually married her, we can still salvage this article."

"Brian, I don't think—"

"Savannah, don't tell me you're losing faith in your abilities. If you can confirm the marriage, the story's worth twice what we talked about before."

"Only twice as much? That's highway robbery, Brian." The words were out before she thought.

"You mean it's worth more than that?" His voice rose suspiciously. "What's up, Savannah? What have you found out?"

"Nothing I can write about." It was true enough, though not in the sense Brian would take it; he would think she meant she had an unconfirmed story that needed just a bit more proof before it was publishable.

Hanging around with Dexter Caine was doing terrible things to her ethical standards, Savannah thought. His ability to say one thing and mean another was turning out to be positively infectious.

Brian was still pestering for details when Savannah heard the front door open. Dexter's home, she thought, with a rush of relief and happiness and anticipation that made her feel almost dizzy.

In the next breath, a little voice at the back of her brain warned that if he caught her talking to a magazine editor she was not apt to like the consequences. "I have to go right now, Brian," she said firmly, and broke the connection while he was still asking where she was and how he could get in touch later.

She rushed out to the atrium before she paused to consider whether it was wise to let Dexter see her in such a hurry. Across the width of the house, he turned at the sound of her footsteps and paused in the act of hanging up his overcoat. "Well, hello," he said softly. "If I didn't know better, I'd think you were anxious to see me."

"There is this little matter of a party tonight." Savannah tried to keep her voice steady, but it trembled a little. "I was afraid you were going to stand me up. If it wasn't for that...."

He smiled and bent to pick up his briefcase and a long sheaf of cellophane, which had been hidden behind it. He'd brought flowers, she realized as he crossed the atrium to hand them to her. She looked down at the glorious armful of yellow and gold and russet and orange, and wondered whether he'd gotten them here in Winter Park, or if he'd brought them all the way from Newark. And if he had, did that mean he'd thought of her often while he was gone?

Dreamer, she accused herself. How would it look for a supposedly newlywed husband not to show up with a bouquet? Dexter might have overlooked the need for rings, but she'd bet her left arm he was experienced enough with women that he never forgot flowers.

"I brought you something else, too," he said, and balanced his briefcase on the stair rail long enough to snap it open and extract a newspaper.

From the size and the type style, Savannah recognized it as one of the wilder tabloids.

"It's a much better picture this time," Dexter warned.

Savannah took a deep breath of floral fragrance for strength and glanced at the front page. He was right; though the picture wasn't particularly flattering, it looked much more like her. If Brian happened to stop at the supermarket tonight on his way home, he wouldn't need to ask why Savannah thought the story of Dexter Caine's reputed wife was a valuable one.

Well, she thought with resignation, she'd expected it after all. She hadn't even dared hope that she'd remain a mystery woman forever until that first bad photo had appeared, and she'd known even then that it was a vain wish.

Funny, though—at the moment it didn't seem to matter. Not while she was standing in that sun-drenched atrium, her hands full of flowers, with Dexter's arm almost around her waist....

"Quite a headline," he added.

"The Honeymooning Caines", Savannah read. Under the photograph the caption noted, *The mystery bride seems a little displeased by our photographer's attentions*. She groaned a little.

"The story says it was too close to deadline to investigate who you are," Dexter said, "but they'll have a better report next week."

He sounded almost gleeful, Savannah thought.

Robinson appeared from the direction of the kitchen. "Good afternoon, sir, and welcome home." He turned to Savannah. "The chef's compliments, Miss Savannah, and he asks what you would like him to serve for dinner after the party."

Dexter's jaw dropped.

"Whatever's easiest," Savannah said. "I'm sure we won't have much appetite anyway, with all the goodies he's making."

Robinson bowed and withdrew.

"What have you done to my staff?" Dexter demanded. "The chef has never asked me what I'd like to eat in the three years he's worked for me."

"Beats me." Savannah wondered what he'd say if dinner turned out to be bratwurst and sauerkraut.

Dexter reached for her left hand and held it up to inspect the rings she wore. "This is certainly an improvement. Sorry, I'm getting ink all over you. Tabloids are messy things in more ways than one, aren't they?"

"Didn't you have someone iron it for you?" Savannah asked sweetly.

"Iron a newspaper? Are you joking?" But his attention had drifted back to her rings. "Did you take these down to the jeweler after all?"

"No. I didn't know if I was allowed."

His eyebrows lifted quizzically. "Allowed? To go out? Do you mean you haven't been outside the house all the time I've been gone? No wonder you look pale."

"I thought—"

"That I was keeping you prisoner? No, my dear."

She considered that for an instant. "You trust me?" Her voice was almost breathless.

"Let's say I trust you to think through the consequences before you act," Dexter murmured. "Besides, someone would have been following you. Let me change my clothes, and we'll go out for a walk, if you like."

She nodded, pretending it was the walk—and not his company—that she wanted.

"I brought you a real present, too," he went on, "but it was too big to carry so it's coming with the luggage. By the time we get back it will be here."

Savannah shook her head a little, but she knew better than to say that the only gift she wanted was him—especially since it was true.

From the instant he'd come in, she'd been trying to ignore her feelings, but suddenly all the longing she'd been trying to fight for the past two days came crashing in upon her with redoubled effect. How was it possible that simply seeing him again could cause this overwhelming pain, this wrenching hunger?

He was watching her, his eyes narrowed. "I missed you, you know," he said finally. "Did you miss me?"

She tried to shake her head, tried to find the words to pass the question off once more as a joke. But instead she mumbled, "Yes."

Dexter's hand came up to cup her chin, and Savannah raised her face and closed her eyes and leaned ever so slightly toward him, starving for the warmth of his body, the strength of his embrace.

His kiss was everything she had been dreaming of for two days. He tasted like sweet wine, like strawberries, like chocolate—every sensual flavor she could think of, mixed into one intoxicating brew that went straight to her head.

He kissed her long and deeply, and when he stopped, Savannah tried to burrow into him, inhaling the wonderful warm scent of his cologne.

He said over her head, "Tell the chef we'll have dinner out this evening, Robinson."

Savannah gave a little moan and tried to push herself away from him, ducking her head so she wouldn't have to look at the butler. She hadn't even heard him return.

Dexter held her firmly. "Are you embarrassed? I'm not." His voice was husky. "But perhaps taking a walk is an even better idea than I thought. A little cold air to the brain might work just as well as an icy shower. I'll be with you in ten minutes, all right?"

He released her and ran up the stairs. Savannah stayed where she was, her hands clenched at her sides, telling herself it was foolish to feel chilly because she no longer was sheltered in the protective warmth of his arms.

Now, more than ever, she must try to keep her head....

But all the arguments she'd had with herself were in vain. She couldn't even remember now all the good reasons she'd assembled for keeping her distance. The only thing she could remember was her desires; the only thing that mattered now was that she loved him.

Even her one remaining question for him no longer haunted her. It didn't really make a difference anymore, whether he could ever care as much about her as she did about him. Perhaps her love would be enough for both, but even if it wasn't, she would take what she could have, for whatever time was left to her. And she would learn to be satisfied with it.

Slowly Savannah climbed the twisting stairs and went into her own room. She had never opened the door in her dressing room that connected with Dexter's suite, though in the past couple of days she'd looked at it often, and curiosity had almost overcome her.

But now her curiosity was banked, sublimated to a far more powerful sensation. She barely noticed the fittings of his dressing room, spare and masculine. She had eyes only for Dexter, with his jacket off, his shirt unbuttoned, in the process of unfastening his cuff links. She leaned against the doorjamb and let her gaze slide over his body as intimately as a touch, enjoying his broad shoulders, lean hips, strong arms....

He caught a glimpse of her in a mirror and paused, his eyebrows lifting slightly.

"Got a match?" she said unsteadily. "I'm in the mood to play with fire."

For a split second, Dexter simply looked at her as if he didn't believe what he was hearing. Then he came across the room to her.

There was a different kind of possessiveness in the way he held her, in the way his lips took hers. There was passion and heat and eagerness—but oddly, no sense of urgency. It was as if their lovemaking was preordained, and there was the rest of time to enjoy each other.

He drew her into his bedroom. Savannah had only a vague impression of massive furniture—shiny black lacquer with oriental accents—before his kisses shut out everything else, and she had no time, no energy, no interest for anything but him.

Making love with him was so effortless, so natural, that she might have done it a hundred times already. But she knew that however often they shared this intimacy, it would never be commonplace; each touch made her long for the next, until her body was vibrating, and only he could soothe the sweet ache of desire and make her whole once more....

For a long while afterward, she lay very still, completely spent, aware of nothing but the warm, sweet aftermath of love and the soft rhythm of his fingers, smoothing her hair back from her temple. They might have been alone in an otherwise abandoned world, without a sound or scent or sight from outside to break their fascination.

Savannah was only dimly aware of minutes passing, of the angle of the sunlight shifting as the afternoon waned, but eventually a vague and inconvenient memory intruded. There was some reason she should care what time it was.

When she stirred to look for a clock, Dexter lazily opened his eyes. "What's the matter?"

"The time," she said.

"It's half past five. Why?"

Savannah sat bolt upright. "Your guests are invited for six!"

He yawned and tried to draw her back into his arms. "I imagine they'll wait for us."

"Of course they'll wait. And what will they be thinking while they're waiting?"

He grinned. "Nothing as wonderful as the truth, if that's what's bothering you. Come here for fifteen more minutes, Savannah."

Savannah was scrambling to gather up her clothes. "Easy for you to say. A quick shower and you're ready. But I'll have to do my makeup and my hair—"

"Personally," Dexter murmured, "I think you're just fine the way you are. You look good when you're slightly disarranged. But I suppose you're going to insist? I should have known I'd regret this idea."

"Why did you want to have a party anyway?"

"Because Robinson confided in me that there's been a continual stream of people coming to the back door ever since you arrived, asking to borrow eggs and sugar and a lot of less likely things, in the hope of getting a glimpse of you."

"Really?"

The corner of his mouth quirked a little. "You're so easily pleased, Savannah, my dear."

She didn't tell him that it wasn't the neighbors' interest in her that she found appealing, but the fact that Robinson had told him of it. Perhaps she'd misjudged Dexter, and he wasn't as unaware of his employees' concerns as he'd appeared. Maybe he wouldn't frown on things like bratwurst and whipped-cream mustaches. And if that was so, was it possible that she might be the kind of woman he wanted after all?

But just now she had no time for contemplation. She fled to her own suite, and a hasty half hour later she dashed down the stairs just as the silver-and-glass grandfather clock struck six.

Dexter was at the foot of the stairs, smiling up at her as she came to him. Privately she thought she had never seen him looking so handsome; his tuxedo was faultless. She straightened his silk jacquard bow tie, more for the chance to touch him than because it needed adjustment.

He had reached for her, as well. His hands rested easily on her hips, holding her just close enough that with every breath he took she could feel the brush of his chest against the thin black crepe of her dress. The soft friction threatened to fan the flames of passion to white heat once more, but Savannah couldn't force herself to step away.

"I'm surprised no one's here yet," she said.

"I imagine they'll be fashionably late, unless even Robinson has underestimated how eager they are to meet you. Your gift has arrived, by the way. Want to see it?"

She almost said no, but he'd already gone to the closet. "You can wear it after the party, when we go to dinner," he said, and brought out a long black velvet evening coat.

She had put the mink jacket out of her mind, but now she remembered it and her eyes sparkled with tears. She knew better than to think she'd converted Dexter to her own opinions about fur, but he'd listened to her, and he respected her feelings—and those things were far more important.

He wrapped the coat around her, and she snuggled her face into the soft depths of the shawl collar. "Dexter, there's something—"

The doorbell rang, and Robinson came across the atrium without hurry to answer it, and then the party was underway and it was too late to say any more.

But perhaps it was just as well, Savannah thought. She needed to think it through before she blurted out things that might be better left forever unsaid.

The party was a blur—a medley of names she would never remember, a collage of faces that all looked the same. Except for Dexter, of course, smiling and relaxed, his eyes still alight with the brilliance of the afternoon. Often she found a gently possessive hand on her arm, or at her waist, as if to tell the world that she was his....

For now, she reminded herself. For right now. That's all you have—and that's all that matters.

One minute, the atrium was full of laughter and music and the click of cocktail glasses, but in the next instant, silence rippled through the room like a shock wave. All over the atrium, heads turned toward the front door.

Automatically, Savannah looked up to see what had caused such a reaction and swallowed a gasp as she saw the woman who stood on the threshold, with Robinson blocking her from entering. A tall woman, with hair so red it couldn't be natural, wearing a floor-length white fur coat.

And just what was Cassie King doing in Winter Park, Savannah wondered, when she was supposed to be on a concert tour?

Cassie tried to push past Robinson; the butler side-stepped and blocked her.

Savannah glanced around the room. Dexter was no-where to be seen, which seemed to leave the problem squarely up to her.

She took a deep breath and started across the room, picking up a fresh glass of champagne from the nearest waiter's tray. "I'll handle this, Robinson," she murmured, and faced the redhead. "You must be Cassie. How good of you to come and wish us happy." She held out the champagne glass, and under her breath she added, "Don't make a fool of yourself, Miss King. It isn't worth it, I promise."

"How nice of you to be concerned about how I look." Cassie's smile was actually more like a snarl. "Though I'm sure you're really more concerned about how you appear. Well, if you expect me to preserve your standing with these people, forget it. See if I care what you look like, you little tramp!" Her voice was rising with every word.

In the doorway just behind Cassie, a man raised a camera to his face, and a photoflash went off before Savannah could react. Half-blinded by the light, she didn't realize Cassie was reaching for the champagne glass she still held, until her wrist turned under the cruel pressure of Cassie's fingers and cold champagne cascaded down the front of Savannah's dress.

The camera flashed again. A gesture from Robinson brought a half-dozen waiters converging on the photographer. Dexter appeared at Savannah's side, pulling out his handkerchief to mop up the mess. Cassie leaned against the door, her arms folded, looking slightly smug.

From the dining-room door a man called, "Mr. Caine! I have to talk to you!"

Savannah knew the voice, but it wasn't until the man made his way through the crowd that she could place him. Then she was even more confused; what was Dexter's former personal assistant doing here? He'd been fired when they were still in Las Vegas.

Dexter said between his teeth, "Not now, Peter. I'm having a party."

"That's why it has to be now, Mr. Caine. Right now. Before anything else happens, you need to know that she's a plant." He jerked a hand at Savannah.

Dexter glared at him. "An orchid, I suppose you mean? Or just a garden-variety chrysanthemum? What the hell are you talking about?"

"She works for the tabloids, Mr. Caine. She wrote the story about Cassie that started this whole thing."

Savannah felt the floor sliding out from under her. It wasn't possible, she thought frantically. No one knew the truth about that story. Not Brian. Not her mother. Not her landlord. Not even the editors of the *Informant* knew her real name....

"One of the *Informant*'s reporters found me, and asked about her," Peter Powell said. "I said I didn't know any more than they did about who the hell Savannah Seabrooke was. But then I started asking questions. I had nothing better to do, since I'd lost my job."

"I told you he'd talk," Savannah said, more to herself than to Dexter.

"I didn't," Peter said hotly. "The reporter called me today as a matter of courtesy and told me who she really is. She used another name, of course. She called herself Brooke Harper, but you can't lie about Social Security numbers."

Savannah wanted to groan. She'd used a pen name and a post office box—but Peter was right; she couldn't manufacture an ID number, so she had used her own. It would never have mattered, because there was no reason for the *Informant* to check who Brooke Harper really was...until now.

"They're going to print the story in tomorrow's edition, Mr. Caine. I came out here to warn you. No doubt she's written the article herself."

Every eye in the house was on Savannah, but the only one she saw was Dexter. There was no judgment in his gaze, and no condemnation—but there was also no reassuring warmth. He was waiting—simply waiting—and the only thing she could do was to tell the truth.

Savannah licked her lips. "It was the only story I ever did for them. I needed the money. I didn't intend...."

She watched the brilliance in his eyes turn to ice, and she felt her heart freeze, too.

CHAPTER TEN

DEXTER'S voice was low and even. "You had a thousand chances to tell me."

Savannah swallowed hard. "I should have. I wanted to."

He shook his head a little in disbelief and started to turn away.

Desperately, she caught at his arm. "Dexter, I did want to tell you, but I thought it would only cause trouble, that it was better to leave it alone."

"Better for whom? For you?"

"For everybody," she whispered. "I thought it was so deeply buried that it could never come out."

"And if you'd realized I would find out before you were safely gone, I suppose you'd have confessed in order to protect yourself."

Savannah felt as if he was slicing little strips off her heart. It wasn't fair how he was twisting things—but it must look to him as if she had kept silent out of self-interest.

"What about the story that's being published to-morrow—the one that announces your position with the tabloid? Did you enjoy writing it, Savannah? Is that what Robinson mailed for you?"

"I had nothing to do with it. I've had no contact with the *Informant* for months, and I was never on the payroll. I wrote one miserable article, that's all."

Cassie cooed, "Trouble in wonderland, Dexter? What a pity!"

Dexter glared at her, one swift, cutting look, and turned back to Savannah. "We'll discuss this later," he said curtly. "Just now, I have guests to entertain."

"And you're doing a wonderful job," Cassie murmured.

I have guests, he'd said. Not *we.*

Now Savannah knew why that anonymous employee had said that a coldly furious Dexter Caine was even more dangerous simply because he was completely in control. It wasn't the champagne still dripping down between her breasts that was making her shiver, but the ice in his voice.

Dexter said, "Go and change, Savannah. I'll deal with you later."

There was not a hint in his voice of the lover who had so tenderly cherished her just hours ago, the man who had so obviously delighted in her body and shared with her the wonders of making love.

"Peter, you'll wait in my office till I'm free," he added coolly.

Savannah turned on her heel. Every eye was on her as she crossed the atrium and climbed the steps, and the click of her heels on the marble floor was the only sound in the room. She felt like an errant child on display before an audience that stood agog, eagerly waiting to see how severe her punishment would be.

She sat down on the edge of her bed, bolt upright, hands folded in her lap, too stunned to care about changing out of her dripping dress. What was the point after all? She certainly wouldn't be going back to the party.

She didn't want to go downstairs and face him again at all, but she supposed there was no choice about that. Dexter would insist, as soon as the party was over. Savannah took a deep breath and tried to find a way to explain the unexplainable.

It had been a difficult summer financially. Few assignments had come her way, and even when she had work, pay had been slow in coming. When Savannah heard about the opportunity to free-lance for the *Informant*, she felt she had to consider it. The money was good, the work didn't look difficult, and if she was careful, she could keep her moonlighting secret and not jeopardize her reputation as a serious reporter and researcher.

So, under the name of Brooke Harper, she had sent a proposal for an article on Cassie King and the woman she'd supposedly saved from dying in a concert hall. Though the *Informant*'s editors hadn't wanted to use that particular idea, they'd asked Savannah to study this sudden new announcement of Cassie's.

But despite Savannah's best efforts to mimic the tabloid's style, her final product had been too restrained and scholarly for the editors' taste. They'd jazzed up the published story, editing out Savannah's careful disclaimers, adding a breathy sort of excitement to the writing, and making the story sound as if the source was a friend of Cassie's instead of careful research.

Savannah hadn't known about the changes till the piece had gone to press, and then it was too late. She was embarrassed about seeing her name—even a made-up name—attached to such a piece of trash. She almost wished they'd gone even farther and wiped out any resemblance to her original, so she could pretend she'd had nothing to do with it.

She'd decided that no amount of money was worth the feeling that she had cheapened her talent by using it in such a cause. So Brooke Harper had never reappeared—in the pages of the *Informant*, or anywhere else—and Savannah had tried her best to forget the entire episode.

On that first morning in Las Vegas, perhaps she'd kept her secret out of self-interest; Dexter already had enough power over her, and it would have been sheer stupidity to give him more ammunition. But as she'd gotten to know him better, she'd begun to feel uneasy about holding back the truth. And when he'd asked how she happened to know so much about how the tabloids worked, the uneasiness had turned into guilt. After that, with every mention of the papers, she'd felt worse.

And she'd told him the truth just now. She had continued to keep quiet day after day because she'd honestly believed that telling him would only hurt him without creating any corresponding good.

This afternoon, however, when she had decided to share her most intimate self with him, she had begun to feel that there was a chance they might build something between them, and perhaps absolute honesty would be best after all. But there had been no time to consider, no time to gently tell him what she'd done. If the party had passed, and he had taken her out for dinner, perhaps....

But it was far too late for that kind of speculation; it only made her heart ache worse to think about the evening they could have shared. And now there was no point in trying to explain, for Dexter would never believe that—mistaken or not—she had truly been thinking of his best interests, not hers.

She wondered what he was likely to do. Would he demand an explanation, or was he likely just to throw her out without bothering? Without a hint of violence, he had already managed to rip her heart from its place. Why should she wait around to find out what else he might have in mind?

She put on her jeans and the dark blue wool blazer she'd been wearing the day—it seemed a million years ago—when she'd walked into Dexter Caine's building on Michigan Avenue. She packed her computer and everything else she'd brought with her in her tote bag. She left the champagne-soaked dress draped across the side of the whirlpool tub, and she didn't spare a glance for any of the other beautiful things Dexter had bought for her. She wouldn't need any kind of souvenir to remember this little trip.

She debated what to do with his grandmother's rings, and finally slipped into Dexter's room—feeling like a sneak thief for being there—and left them cradled on his pillow.

The party was still in progress on the floor below as Savannah slipped silently across the balcony and down the back stairs, thanking heaven for the days of boredom when she'd explored the nooks and crannies of the house. At least she could get out....

Though where she was going, she didn't quite know. She was still stranded in Winter Park after all, and she couldn't imagine hitchhiking through the mountains at night in the cold.

She would have to ask for help. She turned toward the kitchen instead of the back door.

It was obvious from her first glance that the staff knew something dreadful had happened; there were sympathetic glances as she came in, but not a word. Savannah understood that their loyalty had to lie with Dexter. She was a novelty, an aberration—but they must have suspected from the beginning that she wouldn't last.

Robinson was supervising the arrangement of hors d'oeuvres on a row of silver trays. Obviously alerted by the sudden silence, he turned and hurried across the room to her. "Miss Savannah!"

She heard honest surprise in his voice, and it made her want to cry. She lowered her voice. "I don't want to cause trouble, but I need a way to get to Denver. Can you help?"

He studied her for a long moment, and Savannah's heart dropped. "I believe so," he said quietly.

She closed her eyes for an instant in relief. "Perhaps if you tell Mr. Caine that you helped me leave because

I threatened to embarrass him even more if you didn't... maybe he won't blame you that way. He'll believe you didn't want him to be hurt."

"I shall tell the truth, miss," Robinson said firmly.

She was startled, till it occurred to her that perhaps Dexter had already decided not to bother listening to her justifications. He might have told the butler to get her out of the house, and maybe that was why Robinson had been surprised to see her—because he hadn't expected her to make his job easier.

It doesn't matter, she thought. But she couldn't suppress a shiver at the possibility.

"You can't go like that," Robinson said abruptly. "I'll get a coat for you. Do you need money, Miss Savannah?"

She shook her head. "If I can get to Denver, I can manage a plane ticket. My credit card's got a little room on it." Mighty little, she reflected, but she'd worry about that after she was out of Winter Park.

He left the room, and no one spoke for the next five minutes. Savannah might as well have been invisible.

Robinson came back with an oversize parka. "There will be a car at the back door in a moment, Miss Savannah."

She slipped into the coat. Obviously it was his—it was so plain and practical—and suddenly she knew deep inside that this was not part of a scheme of Dexter's to get rid of her, but Robinson's honest desire to help, even if he got into trouble over it. She stuck her hands into the pockets, and her fingertips hit a wad of folded paper. She pulled it partway out and realized it was a bundle of twenty-dollar bills.

"Oh, Robbie—I'm going to miss you." Tears sparkled in her eyes and threatened to overflow. She reached up to kiss his cheek. "I'll pay you back as soon as I can."

His only answer was a sad little smile.

* * *

The photograph stared at Savannah from the supermarket rack. 'Dexter Caine's Mystery Marriage On The Rocks', the headline shrieked. Under the type was the picture of Savannah looking over Cassie King's shoulder directly into the camera, not even reacting yet to the champagne that was sloshing down the front of her dress. 'Wife A Secret Souse', the second headline said.

Savannah bought a copy. Someday she'd no doubt see the humor in all this.

It had been two weeks since she'd fled Winter Park in an old Volkswagen driven by a young man who'd turned out to be Robinson's nephew. He'd told her how delighted he was to be able to do Dexter a favor, however small and indirect it was, in return for the full-tuition scholarship Dexter was providing for him.

He must have thought Savannah looked startled, for—to prove his point—he followed up with a recital of his hero's other good deeds that lasted till they pulled up at the airport in Denver.

It made Savannah's head ache to try to keep all the stories straight; no wonder Dexter's employees were so loyal, for it sounded as if there wasn't one who hadn't been on the receiving end of incredible generosity. But the tales didn't surprise her; she hadn't forgotten the waiter in Las Vegas with the little girl who'd been struck by the car.

The only thing Savannah found amazing, in fact, was that Robinson's nephew spoke so freely about it all. If Dexter ever caught him at it, he'd probably throttle the young man.

But, of course, he'd never hear about it from Savannah, would he?

It had taken most of Robinson's money to get her on board a Chicago-bound flight, and the rest to get from O'Hare into the city, but finally she got home—and in the two weeks since, she'd done her best to get her life back on track. It hadn't been easy.

For the first week there'd been tabloid reporters camped outside the brownstone at all hours. Jack had done his best to protect her, but she didn't blame him for getting tired of the siege. She'd gotten heartily sick of it herself before they finally gave up and went away.

And, of course, when she'd refused to cooperate, the tone of the articles about her had changed. She was no longer the fascinating woman Dexter Caine might have married; now they pictured her as a souse, a tramp, and a schemer.

But that wouldn't last, either, Savannah knew. Sooner or later the interest would die down. In the meantime, she was just trying to get back to normal. She'd scraped up enough money to send Robinson a check, and she'd started work again, though research came hard and she often found herself thinking of Dexter instead of lead poisoning.

Brian, of course, had changed his mind. "Don't waste your talent on lead poisoning," he'd said just this morning when she stopped at *Today's Woman* to drop off the proposal he'd asked for. "Just sit down at the computer over there and tell my readers what really happened, Savannah. We could sell an extra hundred thousand copies next month if you'd tell the inside story. And surely you'd like to have people hear your version of it." Savannah had thanked him politely for the opportunity and walked out, but she was still fuming.

It was a relief to get home to the quiet safety of her little apartment. She still looked around warily before she went in or out, just to be sure no one was lying in wait—but today everything was peaceful, and she unlocked her door and carried her groceries back to the kitchenette. She'd brew a cup of tea and find out what the tabloid had to say about Dexter Caine this week.

It was darned sure that was the only hint of information she'd get, for she hadn't heard a word directly from him. Not that she'd expected to, of course.

She saw the silhouette of a man against the single tiny window in her kitchen, and the bag of groceries slid from her fingers and crashed to the floor. Then she recognized him—more from the way her nerves hummed than from the actual sight. "Dexter? What—how did you get in here?"

He stepped into the light. He was wearing jeans and a dark brown sweater, and she thought he looked bigger and more formidable than ever before. He stooped and started to pick up the mess. "I had a nice chat with your landlord and offered to pay your back rent."

Savannah's jaw dropped. "How did you know about my rent?"

"Jack—that's his name, isn't it?—was still hesitant to let me in, though he looked interested. So I gave him a price he couldn't refuse for the whole building. Now that I own it, he can't keep me out."

Savannah retrieved a carton of eggs. Half of them were broken, but she'd deal with that later. She pushed the carton into the refrigerator. "Send you out for a newspaper in the morning and you'd come back owning the whole *New York Times*," she muttered. She picked up the tabloid and tried to push it unobtrusively behind the cookie jar. It was a foolish move; he couldn't miss seeing the paper. "You really wanted to talk to me, didn't you?" she said. "Okay—what's on your mind?"

"You walked out on me without explaining what happened."

"I walked out? As if it wasn't obvious that I was persona non grata—you didn't really want to talk to me. Besides, I told you everything that matters. A smart guy like you could figure out the rest—if you wanted to." She moved around him to put a loaf of bread away. She was trembling like an aspen leaf in a soft autumn breeze.

"You didn't write the story," he said softly.

"How would you know? Maybe I bought this paper today so I could cut out the pieces I wrote for my scrapbook."

He smiled a little. "If you'd written this trash, you wouldn't have made yourself look so bad. Why didn't you write it, Savannah?"

"Of course I wrote it. That's how writers work things out, Dexter—we put down on paper how we feel. It was very therapeutic."

"What happened? Not even the tabloids believed it?"

She hesitated as she put a container of yogurt in the refrigerator, and something compelled her to tell the truth. "Nobody but me ever saw it." Or ever would, of course. For she hadn't actually constructed a story; she'd simply written down the way she felt about him and everything that had happened—and she could never share that with anyone.

"And did you work it all out?"

"Why would you care? What are you doing here anyway? And why now, just when things are starting to settle down?" She stared at him. "You can't want everything to flare up again, can you?"

"Oh, no. Cassie's been routed, and the tabloids are losing interest, so the worst is over. At least I thought it was, till I chatted with my attorneys last week, and they had what might be termed a hysterical fit."

"Over what?" Savannah said warily.

"Shall we sit down? This might take a while."

"I'd rather not."

"All right." He leaned against the kitchen sink and folded his arms across his chest. "It's a bit technical, though, so bear with me. In the last century when the American frontier was still being settled, there was a lack of certain things that more-developed societies have come to depend on. Things like schools, judges, churches—"

"Is this a conversation or a history lecture?"

"Shush. Since people are only human, they often wanted to establish relationships and families, but since there weren't many preachers, sometimes weddings weren't possible."

"So what?"

"So the concept of common-law marriage was adopted. A couple declared in front of witnesses that they considered themselves married, and that was enough to make it official. Now it's seldom used, of course, but there are places it's still on the books."

Savannah pulled out a chair and abruptly sat down. "And Nevada's one of them?"

The sympathy in his eyes made it clear he'd recognized the understanding—and shock—in hers. "No. But Colorado is."

"And since you referred to me as your wife—" She had to stop to clear her throat. "That means I *am*?"

"My lawyers think it's a very gray area, and suggested it would be prudent to straighten it out."

Savannah put her hands to her temples. "Don't both parties have to declare it intentionally—to be legal, I mean? You said a few things, but I didn't have anything to do with it. I certainly never said we were married—"

"You wore my rings." His voice was low, with a rough edge.

Suddenly Savannah's heart was singing. Could this be real? Was it possible that she truly was his wife? It seemed so crazy, and yet she knew that the common law was full of quirks and twists. If his lawyers believed that a marriage existed, then perhaps it did. And if that was so....

She had just enough sense left to remember that Dexter had sounded anything but thrilled at the prospect. *A gray area... prudent to straighten it out....* His attitude was obvious enough. There was only one reason he was here—he wanted his freedom guaranteed, and he'd come to negotiate some kind of agreement as quickly and quietly as possible.

He's asking for a divorce, she thought helplessly. What an incredible idea that was! She was going to end up divorcing a man she adored, one she would have given her life to marry—if only she'd had the opportunity....

"Better safe than sorry, I suppose you mean." Her tone was like acid, but she told herself that was a lot better than starting to cry. "I seem to remember telling you those rings were a lousy idea."

Silence fell, and for almost a minute neither of them moved. Then Dexter crossed the tiny room and gently put both hands on Savannah's shoulders. "I won't let this injure you, I promise."

She wanted to shrug away from him; it hurt too much to have him touch her without even a hint of the passion they had once shared. "I doubt it's me you're worried about. You got caught, didn't you, Dexter? Your brilliant idea backfired. I wonder how much alimony I could stick you up for."

"Probably not a lot."

"Oh, I don't know." She pushed his hands off her shoulders and stood up, turning to face him. "If you refuse to pay my price, I can always offer to keep the bargain and live with you!"

His hesitation was so brief she almost missed it. "All right. Pack your bags."

For an instant, she let herself dream of going home with him, back to that airy, wonderful house in Winter Park. Or the hotel in Las Vegas. Or anywhere at all—she wouldn't mind, as long as she was with him.

But there had been that hesitation before he spoke, and she knew why—he didn't want her. He was only playing a game of skill—like blackjack or poker. "I admit you're a better bluffer than I am, Dexter. You win." She turned her back so she didn't have to look at him. "I don't want anything. Have your lawyers send me the papers, and I'll sign them—whatever's necessary. And I won't talk, either. Heaven knows I don't want this getting out any more than you do."

"Very well." He seemed disinclined to give any details.

That didn't surprise Savannah, but she didn't understand why, if he had nothing more to say, he didn't just go away. Now that he had what he'd come for, why was he staying?

"Robinson sends his love, by the way," he said quietly, "and his thanks for that ghastly Hawaiian-print shirt you sent him."

Savannah almost managed a smile. She'd tucked the shirt into the package when she returned the butler's coat and his money. "Did he like it? I thought he could use a little color in his life." She took a deep breath. "Maybe you should give me your attorney's address before you go—in case I have a question." If he didn't take that hint to get out, she thought, Dexter was hopeless.

"I'll write it down for you." But he made no move to do so. "You have quite a defender in Robinson, you know. He told me I'd treated you abominably. Which I already knew, of course."

Savannah couldn't force herself to look at him. Tears were starting to sting her eyes, and she was terrified that at any second she was going to burst into noisy sobs like a heartbroken child. She swallowed hard. "There's no point in going over this, Dexter. Handle the whole mess however you think best."

"All right. I will." She heard his footsteps on the hardwood floor, and she braced herself for the moment when she would hear him no longer, when the last trace of him would vanish forever from her life and all that was left would be the paperwork, cold and impersonal.

Then he said, almost into her ear, "Is there any way you'd consider letting this stand, Savannah?"

She gasped, then choked. She must be hearing things; he couldn't actually be saying that he *wanted* to be married!

His hands came to rest softly, almost tentatively, on her shoulders. "It was quite a blow to me when Peter dropped his little bombshell," Dexter said softly. "I've never encountered anyone so open and warm and giving as you, and I thought I knew you all the way through. But when I realized you had hidden such a very important part of your life—I didn't take it very well. If you had hidden that from me, what else didn't I know?"

She tried to tell him there was nothing, but she couldn't form the words; she could do no more than shake her head.

"I was confused and hurt, and there wasn't time to sort it all out because you ran away. It was only later, after you were gone and I'd had a chance to think, that I understood the trap you'd been caught in." He turned her slowly to face him.

Did he understand? Was it possible that he could forgive her one colossal error? Cautiously, afraid of what she would see in his face, Savannah raised her eyes.

"If you didn't tell me," he went on, "the secret might explode in your face some day. If you did, there was no doubt. It would have blown up right then—and anything we shared would have gone up in smoke right along with it."

Dawning wonder clutched at her heart.

"Am I right, Savannah? Do we share...something? I don't think I can be wrong—our minds fit like gears, and our bodies.... What happened to us that afternoon doesn't happen to everyone, you know."

"I know." She held out her arms to him, and for a long time there was no need for words.

When finally he stopped kissing her, it was only to lead her into the small living room. She curled up next to him on the couch and put her face on his chest so she could treasure the slowly steadying beat of his heart.

"I took you to Winter Park because it was driving me crazy to be so close to you in that little hotel suite and not make love to you," he confessed. "Even that first night, I didn't want to leave you. I didn't know why—"

"I do," Savannah murmured. "It was lust."

Dexter smiled. "Well, maybe a little. I didn't expect to walk in and find a fire storm waiting in my extra bedroom."

"I didn't start that, Dexter. I'm absolutely positive I didn't kiss you first."

"You certainly did. I leaned over to wake you, and you pulled me down beside you and.... Look, Savannah, if I promise not to tell our children, will you at least admit it?"

"Children?" There was a catch in her throat at the very thought of his children. *Their* children.

He was running his fingers through her hair, drawing the long blond strands out into a complex pattern across the shoulder of his sweater. "When I looked at you across the table that night when the photographer asked who you were, and started to give your name, and 'Mrs. Caine' just popped out—"

"Then you didn't plan that announcement?"

"Do I strike you as crazy? Of course I didn't plan it. Even while I was saying it, I knew it made no sense to take a risk like that. There wasn't a reason in the world I should trust you—and you didn't make things any better afterward, either. For the next week, every time you opened your mouth it seemed you were reminding me that you weren't planning to honor your promise."

"I would have kept my word," she murmured. "I just didn't want you to know that. It scared me too much even to think that you were more important than the story was. To have told you that—"

"I feel much better," Dexter murmured. "You see, I thought I'd really lost my mind. That idiot reporter asked his question, and suddenly I could see the two of us together—laughing, making love, raising children, growing old.... And the name just slipped out."

Savannah looked up at him and smiled and whispered, "I love you, Dexter." A long while later, she pressed a kiss at the base of his throat and said, "While I'm thinking about it, did Robinson really dare to tell you you'd treated me badly?"

"Oh, yes. Then he followed up by announcing that I was acting like a bear with a sore paw, and told me the staff at the house in Sydney were so tired of my behavior they were trying to get me to leave."

"Sydney? You've been in Australia?"

He slanted an ironic look down at her. "I suppose I could have gone to the Himalayas and been a little farther from you, but, as I think I told you once, I happen to like my creature comforts. After the staff made Sydney too uncomfortable, I went to Ireland, but the very day I arrived, the housekeeper politely asked when she'd get to meet you. At that point I'd have bought a ticket for Mars, but I didn't think it would be far enough away, either, so I came back here and talked to the lawyers."

"Would you have come if it hadn't been for them?" Savannah whispered.

He smiled. "Oh, yes."

Savannah didn't even realize she'd had one last tiny, nagging twinge of doubt until she saw the warmth in his eyes and knew that no matter what the circumstances he was truly content.

Dexter kissed her temple and mused, "I think we should drive down to Urbana this afternoon—or maybe tomorrow—so I can meet your mother. Besides, I'm sure she'll have some opinions about the wedding plans."

It took an instant for that to register, and then Savannah sat straight up in his arms. "Wedding plans?

Do you mean all that stuff about a common-law marriage was so much malarkey? Dexter Caine—"

"No, it wasn't malarkey. Well, not exactly. When I brought up the subject of common-law marriage with the lawyers—"

"*You* brought it up?"

"They did say it's a very gray area, and I believe it's the height of foolishness to pay for advice and then not take it, even if I did have to prod them a bit before they got concerned. So just in case we haven't managed to meet the technicalities, I want everything tied up properly, complete with a marriage license framed and hung over our bed."

She blinked. "All of them? Beds, I mean. How many do you have anyway?"

Dexter grinned. "A whole lot. Why shouldn't we have a license for each one? I suspect I'm going to like getting married, and if it extends the honeymoon, I'm all for it. Now that Peter's back to work, I can relax a bit."

"Whatever you say," she murmured. "As long as it's official soon. Oh, there's just one more thing. You said you'd routed Cassie. How did you manage that?"

"Easy. I told her if she kept it up, you'd start writing for the tabloids again, specializing in her. With your connections and information, we could keep her on the hot seat for years, even if I have to buy the damned paper to do it. It was amazing how quickly she decided to be reasonable. Yes," he mused, "you're absolutely the most wonderful woman in the world for me. You even have the perfect job—you can free-lance from anywhere."

Savannah peeked up at him through her lashes. "Can I write your biography after all?"

Dexter frowned. "The inside story of my life? You can't mean you still want to."

"Oh, yes I do. Of course, I'll need a lot more research first." Her fingertips wandered up his throat and around his neck to tug his face down to hers. "A lifetime's worth, I expect."

"Starting right now, I suppose?" Dexter smiled and drew her closer. "Sounds just fine to me. Where would you like to begin?"

RUGGED. SEXY. HEROIC.

Stony Carlton—A lone wolf determined never to be
tied down.

Gabriel Taylor—Accused and found guilty by
small-town gossip.

Clay Barker—At Revenge Unlimited, he *is* the law.

JOAN JOHNSTON, DALLAS SCHULZE and
MALLORY RUSH, three of romance fiction's
biggest names, have created three unforgettable
men—modern heroes who have the courage to fight
for what is right....

OUTLAWS AND HEROES—available in September
wherever Harlequin books are sold.

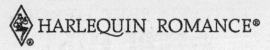

HARLEQUIN ROMANCE®

brings you

Romances that take the family to heart!

A FAMILY CLOSENESS by Emma Richmond

If Davina's fiancé hadn't run off with her best friend, she wouldn't have got involved with Joel Gilman. And now, four years after their disastrous encounter, it seemed that time hadn't dulled their mutual attraction! But Joel had a new woman in his life now—his young daughter, Ammy. And when he asked her to look after the little girl, Davina had a temporary chance to experience what might have been—and what she'd always wanted....

**Coming next month, from the bestselling author of
MORE THAN A DREAM!**

FT-3

FLYAWAY VACATION SWEEPSTAKES!

This month's destination:

Glamorous LAS VEGAS!

Are you the lucky person who will win a free trip to Las Vegas? Think how much fun it would be to visit world-famous casinos... to see star-studded shows...to enjoy round-the-clock action in the city that never sleeps!

The facing page contains two Official Entry Coupons, as does each of the other books you received this shipment. Complete and return all the entry coupons—**the more times you enter, the better your chances of winning!**

Then keep your fingers crossed, because you'll find out by August 15, 1995 if you're the winner! If you are, here's what you'll get:

- Round-trip airfare for two to exciting Las Vegas!
- 4 days/3 nights at a fabulous first-class hotel!
- $500.00 pocket money for meals and entertainment!

Remember: The more times you enter, the better your chances of winning!*

*NO PURCHASE OR OBLIGATION TO CONTINUE BEING A SUBSCRIBER NECESSARY TO ENTER. SEE REVERSE SIDE OF ANY ENTRY COUPON FOR ALTERNATIVE MEANS OF ENTRY.

VLV KAL

FLYAWAY VACATION
SWEEPSTAKES
OFFICIAL ENTRY COUPON

This entry must be received by: JULY 30, 1995
This month's winner will be notified by: AUGUST 15, 1995
Trip must be taken between: SEPTEMBER 30, 1995-SEPTEMBER 30, 1996

YES, I want to win a vacation for two in Las Vegas. I understand the prize includes round-trip airfare, first-class hotel and $500.00 spending money. Please let me know if I'm the winner!

Name_____

Address _____ Apt. _____

City   State/Prov.   Zip/Postal Code

Account #_____

Return entry with invoice in reply envelope.

© 1995 HARLEQUIN ENTERPRISES LTD.   CLV KAL

FLYAWAY VACATION
SWEEPSTAKES
OFFICIAL ENTRY COUPON

This entry must be received by: JULY 30, 1995
This month's winner will be notified by: AUGUST 15, 1995
Trip must be taken between: SEPTEMBER 30, 1995-SEPTEMBER 30, 1996

YES, I want to win a vacation for two in Las Vegas. I understand the prize includes round-trip airfare, first-class hotel and $500.00 spending money. Please let me know if I'm the winner!

Name_____

Address _____ Apt. _____

City   State/Prov.   Zip/Postal Code

Account #_____

Return entry with invoice in reply envelope.

© 1995 HARLEQUIN ENTERPRISES LTD.   CLV KAL

OFFICIAL RULES

FLYAWAY VACATION SWEEPSTAKES 3449

NO PURCHASE OR OBLIGATION NECESSARY

Three Harlequin Reader Service 1995 shipments will contain respectively, coupons for entry into three different prize drawings, one for a trip for two to San Francisco, another for a trip for two to Las Vegas and the third for a trip for two to Orlando, Florida. To enter any drawing using an Entry Coupon, simply complete and mail according to directions.

There is no obligation to continue using the Reader Service to enter and be eligible for any prize drawing. You may also enter any drawing by hand printing the words "Flyaway Vacation," your name and address on a 3"x5" card and the destination of the prize you wish that entry to be considered for (i.e., San Francisco trip, Las Vegas trip or Orlando trip). Send your 3"x5" entries via first-class mail (limit: one entry per envelope) to: Flyaway Vacation Sweepstakes 3449, c/o Prize Destination you wish that entry to be considered for, P.O. Box 1315, Buffalo, NY 14269-1315, USA or P.O. Box 610, Fort Erie, Ontario L2A 5X3, Canada.

To be eligible for the San Francisco trip, entries must be received by 5/30/95; for the Las Vegas trip, 7/30/95; and for the Orlando trip, 9/30/95.

Winners will be determined in random drawings conducted under the supervision of D.L. Blair, Inc., an independent judging organization whose decisions are final, from among all eligible entries received for that drawing. San Francisco trip prize includes round-trip airfare for two, 4-day/3-night weekend accommodations at a first-class hotel, and $500 in cash (trip must be taken between 7/30/95—7/30/96, approximate prize value—$3,500); Las Vegas trip includes round-trip airfare for two, 4-day/3-night weekend accommodations at a first-class hotel, and $600 in cash (trip must be taken between 9/30/95—9/30/96, approximate prize value—$3,500); Orlando trip includes round-trip airfare for two, 4-day/3-night weekend accommodations at a first-class hotel, and $500 in cash (trip must be taken between 11/30/95—11/30/96, approximate prize value—$3,500). All travelers must sign and return a Release of Liability prior to travel. Hotel accommodations and flights are subject to accommodation and schedule availability. Sweepstakes open to residents of the U.S. (except Puerto Rico) and Canada, 18 years of age or older. Employees and immediate family members of Harlequin Enterprises, Ltd., D.L. Blair, Inc., their affiliates, subsidiaries and all other agencies, entities and persons connected with the use, marketing or conduct of this sweepstakes are not eligible. Odds of winning a prize are dependent upon the number of eligible entries received for that drawing. Prize drawing and winner notification for each drawing will occur no later than 15 days after deadline for entry eligibility for that drawing. Limit: one prize to an individual, family or organization. All applicable laws and regulations apply. Sweepstakes offer void wherever prohibited by law. Any litigation within the province of Quebec respecting the conduct and awarding of the prizes in this sweepstakes must be submitted to the Regies des loteries et Courses du Quebec. In order to win a prize, residents of Canada will be required to correctly answer a time-limited arithmetical skill-testing question. Value of prizes are in U.S. currency.

Winners will be obligated to sign and return an Affidavit of Eligibility within 30 days of notification. In the event of noncompliance within this time period, prize may not be awarded. If any prize or prize notification is returned as undeliverable, that prize will not be awarded. By acceptance of a prize, winner consents to use of his/her name, photograph or other likeness for purposes of advertising, trade and promotion on behalf of Harlequin Enterprises, Ltd., without further compensation, unless prohibited by law.

For the names of prizewinners (available after 12/31/95), send a self-addressed, stamped envelope to: Flyaway Vacation Sweepstakes 3449 Winners, P.O. Box 4200, Blair, NE 68009.

RVC KAL